AF378521

Holding
Out

crocus

crocus

Holding Out

SHORT
STORIES
by
WOMEN

First published in 1988 by Crocus.

Crocus books are published by

Commonword Ltd,
Cheetwood House,
21 Newton Street,
Manchester, M1 1FZ.

© 1988 Commonword Ltd and the Authors

No part of this publication may be reproduced without written permission, except in the case of brief extracts embodied in critical articles, reviews or lectures. For information contact Commonword Ltd.

Commonword gratefully acknowledge financial assistance from the Association of Greater Manchester Authorities, North West Arts, Manchester City Council and the Commission for Racial Equality.

Typeset and printed by RAP Ltd, Rochdale, OL12 7AF

British Library Cataloguing in Publication Data

Holding Out.
  1. Short stories in English. Women writers, 1945--Anthologies.
  823'.01'089287 [FS].

ISBN 0 946745 30 7

Contents

Introduction

We were delighted by the response from women writers when we advertised for short stories two years ago. We received up to seventy stories, such that an editorial group was set up involving ten women, who spent many hours sifting through the manuscripts, commenting on each one in turn, never ceasing to be impressed, surprised and concerned by the issues affecting the lives of the women depicted in these stories.

Share with these new writers a whole range of women's experiences, the strengths and dreams, the hardships and abuse. HOLDING OUT contains stories to delight and thrill, to inform and shock. Chilling stories exposing the depths of isolation, of fears and insecurity, like *Bereavement*. Gripping stories such as *The Discovery*, where the conflict between a young Asian couple leads to unresolved tensions. Bizarre stories, leaping into the absurd with *News Items*.

The possibility of identifying with the women characterized in HOLDING OUT is, you will no doubt agree, both unsettling and relieving. What are women writing about in the late 1980's? How do their conditions of life affect their aspirations and mirth? How desperate will a young mother get, wholly demoralized by an insensitive and callous husband? Perhaps it will take *15 Seconds* to illustrate this.

At the same time there is plenty of sweet happiness around these courageous women, writing in the 1980's, wishing to pursue personal interest and success with music, comedy and love. Exploring relationships with women and men, without the fear of rape, restriction or rebuff, detailed in such pieces as: *Andante; Over Here; Comic Cuts;* and *I'll Know My Song Well.*

HOLDING OUT invites you to enter the eccentricities of individuality and flippancy, with *A New Bra; The Little*

Looker; and *Still Life.* In HOLDING OUT you will find stories spanning the age range; from birth, childhood, womanhood, to the older aged woman.

In HOLDING OUT there is also anger. From women who are being dealt the most debilitating blows of disappointment, male brutality, racism, incest, poverty and isolation. Sometimes there is also unexplicably repressed frustration. In the *Confinement* a woman can get delightful repose from her many children after a tragic still birth. Or, as in *A Day of Rest*, can be trapped within a hateful marriage of brutality.

The writing of women today reflects vividly the variations of strength, will and happiness. The strength of women's friendships and joys shared together, the will to remain true to oneself and not be swayed or demoralized by reactionary culture, sexist men or mundanity, of women's endurance at any age; when looking at the pressures of an unwanted pregnancy in *Third Time Lucky*; of the anxiety of crossing two cultures as in *A Pair of Jeans*; and of child sex abuse as in *Daddy's Toy.*

There is something in HOLDING OUT for all women, not easy answers or solutions, not raising too many questions, stories wishing to entertain you and to tell you quite a lot too. Most importantly though, this collection of short stories illustrates that women whatever their everyday circumstances, are holding out.

As an editorial group we were looking for a good balance of writing, importantly expressing and representing the lives of all women's feelings and experiences in Britain today. Stories for the young woman, and the older woman, black woman and white woman, strong and weak, happy and angry. We recognise the dearth in the publishing world in written form of the experiences of all women. We hope you will enjoy this selection of ours.

The New Bra

Liz Tolan

I am wondering if it is worthwhile buying myself a new bra. Will I live long enough to make good use of it. For that matter what do I want or need one for? Well — its warmth and comfort — yes, a safety harness. At my age. I am not interested in presenting myself as an object for admiration or desire. My breasts are small. They fluctuated with pregnancy and suckling, but were always small. They do not need holding up as such.

I am mortal. I have been dying for thirty years. Ever since Mother's long death when I suddenly became conscious of my body living, breathing, pulsing, beating, and simultaneously fearful of it stopping. Before that, death had not touched me, but ever since, I have been aware of it as a natural event. From then on death was all around and life was merely evasion of death.

A natural reaction to this realization would have been to adopt the pleasure principle and live for the moment. But this was so contrary to my nature and upbringing that I could not do it. I continued to live as if life were guaranteed. I did my duty. All my pleasures were deserved.

Should I buy the bra? What else have I to spend my money on? There isn't a lot to spare but I have enough coal to last the winter. My son sent me a cheque at Christmas. 'Treat yourself, Mother.' So I stocked up the coal place. They were here last summer. Stopped overnight on their way to somewhere else. Two large teenagers slept on the floor. My Grandchildren.

If I run short of coal, if the Spring is a cold one, I could eke it out with wood. I am seriously thinking of chopping up the heavy, lugubrious — yes, lugubrious — sideboard that was a wedding present. Solid oak. Hard wood. It would burn slowly. Or perhaps not, being so dry. And the years of polish rubbed into its surface. But I would need someone to take an axe to it. Who could I ask? Who would do such a thing for an old woman? 'Finish off the sideboard, please finish it off ...' 'Oh but we couldn't, couldn't do such a thing.'

I hated the sideboard the minute I saw it. His Mother chose it for my home. Its heavy faces and flat feet. I wanted something delicate, light.

A large pale bird has landed at the bottom of the garden, plump and fluffed up. I can't identify it. It's too far away. But It is certainly not a sparrow, starling, blackbird, magpie, pigeon. Maybe it's a thrush but it looks too light in colour. The colour of a Jersey cow — café au lait.

Café au lait was one of the exotic titles used for colours in the mail order office. Ecru was another. Ecru was a popular shade for ladies jumpers in nylon and acrilan newly discovered. I worked there with Barbara and her red finger-nails. For years on end. Flicking through files. Noting down colours available — ecru, bottle, navy, plum. Pastel pink and blue. Barbara's fingers flashed beside me and her cigarette smoke curled up my nose.

She's dead, now. Dead and cold and forever fixed at forty-nine. And I was left to continue flicking the pages with so-meone new beside me. A succession of girls accompanied by my bereavement. None of them stayed. Girls with inno-cent eyes that soon clouded over with knowledge of life and love.

Gradually I can burn up all my household effects. Save them a job when I'm gone. Save the carting away by some second-hand trader to be sold to furnish gloomy bedsitters or the back to back homes of young couples. Damp and leaky. Bronchitic baby. Waiting for a council house.

The useless articles inside the furniture can go to jumble sales or into the dustbin. The china tea service, the best cutlery, the ornaments. Drawers of letters and postcards and photographs. I have no use for them. I am unsentimental. The old are unsentimental. And I am old. I could keep them for the children, but why? The photographs are black and white and have no connection with the coloured lives recorded in their snaps (though these will fade with time, everything will become yellow tinted, jaundiced). Aunt Edith's stern studio smile. Ideal for burning.

I will pare down to the essentials. I need so little. And then — then will buy a new bra. Not the most sensible, or cheapest, or easily laundered, but light and frivolous with a blue bow or peach embroidery or delicate lace. Maybe in ecru or café au lait. But not navy, bottle or plum.

Over Here

Kate Thomas

She didn't want to go. She'd been dreading it all day, it had entirely spoilt her Saturday. There were at least a thousand other things she could think of that she'd rather do. Her resentment grew slowly on her journey, and by the time she approached the doors it was almost anger of a slow, sullen kind.

Well, here she was, anyway.

She pushed open the shiny chrome and plate glass door of the Dreamburger Company and the stale smell of fried food hit her first, like it always did. Everything in the restaurant smelled like a greasy burger; she came out of there every day smelling like a greasy burger; every evening she scrubbed and scrubbed, trying to wash the smell off her body, out of her hair, but she was sure it lingered. She felt as if she exuded it. Burger Odour she called it, the new anti-social smell. In slack moments at the Dreamburger Company she and the other girls made up adverts for 'Burger Off', the fast and effective way to deal with that embarrassing fast food odour.

In the wash room she put on her uniform and felt obliterated by it. She looked in the mirror and couldn't see herself, only the brown overall and the bloody silly little hat.

'What's up, Marilyn,' asked the girl pinning on her hat next to her. 'You look really pissed off.'

'Saturday late shift. Do you blame me?'

'No, not really' said the girl looking at the floor. 'Still,' she said 'it's a job.'

'Yes' said Marilyn, 'I suppose it is.'

Although she'd been busy all night, the hands on the clock

seemed to be creaking round so slowly it was almost painful. They had reached half past eleven now, but she felt as if she'd been there for centuries. Only half an hour to go till freedom now, though, and the rush of customers was dying down.

Her face ached from the compulsory Dreamburger Company smile that she served up with every order, and she felt tired. She'd only been working at the restaurant for six months, but it seemed like years. When she thought how thrilled she'd been to start the job, her first real job, it made her feel jaded. It was better than the dole, perhaps, at least she was doing something. But she felt cheated, somehow. She couldn't believe that this was all there was, and was sure that somehow, somewhere along the line she'd been subtly promised something different, something more; she wanted that something more, and intended to have it. The problem was, she wasn't even sure what it was. Her family seemed to think that marriage and babies were the answer, but from what Marilyn had seen of this amongst her friends, she wasn't so sure. One thing she was sure about was that working in this bloody place until she got promoted to supervisor wasn't the answer either. Even supervisor went home smelling of greasy burgers.

As she mused on these thoughts she watched a teenage boy playing on the games machine near the counter. It was a new machine, one that the manager seemed to think was very witty. In the game you were a little red dot, and you were chased round a maze by burgers that opened and shut like snapping mouths. You had to try to destroy them by shooting them down with squirts of bright red ketchup, but every so often a new one would appear out of nowhere, and it was only a matter of time before they had you surrounded. Then no amount of ketchup missiles could save you from being gobbled up by them.

The machine gave Marilyn nightmares, and she was almost glad when a sudden wave of customers diverted her attention from it.

Although she was busy, she noticed him the moment he walked into the restaurant.

She noticed him because he seemed more real than

everybody around him. His movements, the lines of his body, were strong and definite; he was all bright, true colours, from the blue of his eyes and his perfectly fitted jeans, to the gold of his skin and his cropped hair to the bright white of his tee-shirt and of oh, when it came, of that smile.

He took a packet of Marlboros out of the red baseball jacket that slung casually over one broad shoulder. Lighting a cigarette, he studied the menu on the wall above Marilyn's head. After exchanging a few words with his companions he strolled over to queue at her till.

The queue was long, and by the time it was his turn to order, she was a wreck. As he came close to the counter she was sure that his force field surrounded her. She could feel it. Then came the smile that was like a blast, and she could only take it all by keeping quite still and relaxing. If she did not relax, she told herself, some vital part of her would short circuit and render her incapable of speech or action.

He gave his order. She took the low tones, the flowing rhythm, the soft American accent. But the sense of the words escaped her entirely.

Silence.

'Can you repeat that, please?'

'Three Burgers, two Fries, one chocolate shake and two cokes,' he said, without a hint of impatience.

He paid her, and she managed, somehow, to get the order together. With a final blast of the smile he took it and said 'thanks', lingered for a fraction of a second just looking at her, then collected his companions and left.

Out of his force field she was once more a capable human being, energised in fact, by the contact with him.

This, she decided, was reality.

The next night he was back; alone this time. He walked straight up to her till and said 'Hi' and the force field closed around her again.

'A Burger and a coke, please,' he said.

'Anything else?' The words came out of her mouth, but she didn't know where from. As she looked at him she realised he had put them there as a cue.

'Yes,' he replied. 'I'd like a date.'

She nodded her consent slowly. He suggested a time and a place, and again she nodded, her eyes held, all the time by his gaze. He asked her name. His name was Kurt, he informed her. Then he said goodbye and releasing her from his presence, was gone.

Sitting on the bus on the way home she abandoned herself to the luxury of daydreams. They were driving along in a car and she looked glamorous in a red dress and high heeled red shoes, with the breeze from the open window ruffling her hair. When he turned to look at her she gave him a dazzling Monroe smile, and he found it hard to turn his eyes back to the road.

They were driving down long dusty roads in a beaten up old Ford, and he was being intense like James Dean, and she had to try to understand him because no one else did; or else they were in a flashy, tacky, souped up Cadillac, driving through town on a Saturday afternoon, and he was being moody like Elvis, but this was easier because she knew it would all end with a song; or perhaps they were driving through a busy city at night, with bright lights all around them, in a chauffeur driven limousine, and it was all very restrained. He was very formal and sophisticated, like Cary Grant but she could tell how much he wanted her underneath the formality, and ... She realised it was her stop and clattered down the stairs of the bus.

On Tuesday night she prepared herself carefully for the evening. After a long bath and a stolen puff of her mum's best perfume, she set out to work on her face. She smoothed on pale foundation cream all over her face; lightened her eyelids; darkened the sockets, blackened the lashes. She drew on two arched eyebrows and shaded her cheekbones. Then a glossy bright red pout of a mouth, and she was finished.

She smiled into the mirror at the face she had created and fluffed out her freshly dyed silvery white hair. She was ready

She arrived a little late, on purpose, and he was sitting there at the bar, so sharp edged that everything around him seemed dingy and lifeless. When she said 'Hello' he turned the full force of his smile onto her and said 'Hi, Marilyn,' and she had to sit down.

He ordered her a vodka and coke, and pointing to a copy of 'City Life' open on the bar in front of him said 'What movie are you into?' She looked at the page but the words kept jumping around and running into one another, and she couldn't focus. God, she hoped she didn't look as nervous as she felt.

Taking a gulp of her drink, she smiled the smile she'd practised in the mirror, although it felt more like a frightened grimace, and said 'You choose.'

'Well, let's see. There's 'A Letter to Brezhnev'.'

'Yes, that sounds really good. I haven't seen it yet.'

'Yeah,' he said 'It's about Manchester isn't it?'

'Er, no, Liverpool,' she said, and immediately felt unsophisticated for enthusing about it.

Then he suggested that they see 'Gremlins', and she laughed, thinking he was joking. He looked slightly offended, and she realised that she'd messed that one up, too. She'd agree to the next suggestion, whatever it was.

'Now here's something,' he said. 'How about 'Easy Rider'?'

She must have looked blank, because he showed her the piece about it in the magazine. The date of the film caught her attention; 1969, the year she was born.

'Sounds fine', she said.

'Oh, it's a great movie,' he replied. 'I've seen it three times. Hey, we'd better move, it starts in ten minutes.' He gulped down his scotch and they left.

As they queued for tickets, she looked at a poster for 'The Killing Fields' which was also on at the cinema.

'Have you seen it?' she asked, pointing to the poster.

'Yeah', he said, and looked slightly uneasy. 'There's some good camera work in it. Have you?'

She shook her head.

'I don't like violent films,' she said.

'There's a little violence in 'Easy Rider',' he said 'But only a little, and it's right at the end. I'll warn you when it's going to come and you can look away.'

'Thanks,' she said, and he smiled at her protectively.

As they came out of the cinema, blinking and trying to

re-adjust from Tennessee sunshine to Manchester rain, he asked her if she'd enjoyed the film.

'Yes,' she said. 'Did they die at the end?' She hadn't seen
the last part of the film because he'd taken hold of her hand
and said 'Don't look now', and with his other hand had gently pulled her head towards his shoulder; so when the gun
shots rang out, all she had been able to see was the dazzling
white of his tee-shirt.

'Yeah', he said 'They died. But the rest of it was really
beautiful, wasn't it? Europeans don't think of America as
beautiful,' he added, warming to his subject 'they think it's
just big cities, like New York. But it's not.'

'I think of it as beautiful,' she said. 'But the cities too.
Especially New York.'

He laughed. 'I think you'd be disappointed there,' he said.
'New York's not very pretty.'

'But it's exciting, though, isn't it?'

'It certainly is.'

'Well that's enough, then.'

He laughed again, and said 'Well, I'm a Californian, so
maybe I'm biased.'

She thought of California, and images of beaches and
surfers and Hollywood glamour came to mind.

'Is it beautiful there too?' she asked.

'California,' he said 'is the most beautiful place on God's
earth.'

'Oh,' she said. 'That's nice.'

'Seeing that Yank again, are you?' asked her father as
Marilyn drifted into the sitting room and glanced hopefully
out of the window.

'His name's Kurt, Dad.'

'Humph. I don't know what's wrong with English lads.
You'll end up like your Auntie Vera.'

Marilyn's Auntie Vera had caused a scandal in the family
during the war by becoming engaged to a GI, and announc-
ing that she was going to marry him and go and live in Texas.
Her plans were thwarted, however, when it was discovered
that her fiance was in fact already married and the father
of three children. She had never got over the disappointment,

and was still reduced to tears every time she heard 'We'll Meet Again' being played. The rest of the family regarded her as ridiculously sentimental but Marilyn secretly thought it was all very romantic.

'Are you sure this Yank of yours isn't married?' her father continued.

'Yes, Dad.'

'Some of them are into this bigamy lark, aren't they?'

'Only Mormons, Dad.'

'And he's not one of them, then.'

'No, Dad.'

'Humph. Still can't see what's wrong with English lads', he said, but was drowned out by the loud hooting of a car horn outside.

'That'll be Kurt. See you Dad. Bye Mum.'

'Have a nice time, love', her mother called from the kitchen, and Marilyn rushed out slamming the door.

'He's a nice looking lad, that American of hers,' said Marilyn's mother, as she came into the living room, drying her hands in a teatowel, her eyes fixed on the window. 'Not short of a bob or two either, by the looks of that car.' She watched her daughter get into the car and drive off. She sighed. 'It's a pity he's not a Catholic', she said.

'Aye, I wish that was all that was wrong with him', muttered Marilyn's father, darkly.

It was Sunday afternoon and they were lazing around in Kurt's flat. Or apartment, as he called it, which Marilyn thought was a much nicer word. She liked the apartment; it was big and airy and had enormous windows that looked out onto a park. She liked the tranquility of the rooms, the sense of effortless order; the way everything had a place, and was in it. Not like her home, where her mother practiced her own brand of quiet anarchy, where despite the apparent neatness of the house, you felt that objects were in a state of constant motion. You never knew where anything was likely to be. Even the furniture was re-arranged regularly. Or rather irregularly, when you least expected it. This unsettled Marilyn. She had made a small attempt to impose some sort of order by buying her mother a set of canisters marked 'Tea', 'Coffee', 'Sugar', 'Flour', and 'Biscuits', but this failed to restrain Mrs Dolan, who merely flouted the labels and proceeded to keep anything she fancied in the various tins, much to Marilyn's horror. She found currants in the coffee tin, bills in the biscuit tin, make-up in the tea tin. Once she even found sugar in the sugar tin, which she thought was the crowning irony, a kind of two fingers up in the face of order itself, declaring it to be just one permutation of chaos.

In Kurt's flat, however, you knew what to expect. There would be sugar in the sugar cannister, and nothing else (and it would never be empty). She found this enormously comforting, and would sometimes wander from room to room, drinking in the way everything was in exactly the same place as it always had been, and always would be. She felt safe.

She felt particularly safe that afternoon, as she lay there on the settee, wrapped in Kurt's dressing gown. She was attached to this dressing gown. It was blue and had 'Wrangler' written on the pocket in yellow, and was one of the many perks Kurt got from working for an advertising agency. She envied him these free gifts; it must be nice, she thought, to get something for nothing.

She lay there now feeling cocooned and happy. They had been making lazy love all afternoon, and then she'd cooked them a huge meal. Now they were lying around like cats in the sun, self-indulgent and satisfied. Everything, Marilyn thought, was the way it should be.

Kurt was scanning the TV pages in the paper. He looked up and said 'Hey, there's a Western on. We've only missed five minutes of it.'

He pressed the remote control switch and a Wild West scenario sprung up in front of them.

Horses were pulling a stage coach along a track, and the stagecoach was full of people wearing stiff, uncomfortable clothes and looking anxious and expectant. Some more horses appeared, with Red Indians riding on them, and they began to circle the stagecoach. The Red Indians fired arrows into the coach, and the men inside fired guns out at the Indians. In a close-up of one of the Red Indians, showing him dragging the coach driver from his seat and sinking a small hatchet into the back of his skull, Marilyn noticed that the

Indian's make-up had streaked slightly under the lights, exposing a white skin under the red surface.

This seemed strange to her; she'd always assumed that the Red Indians she saw on the screen were real Red Indians. She found it ludicrous when she thought that white men dressed up as cowboys or cavalrymen or settlers and other white men painted their skins red and dressed up as Indian Braves and they all went through this battle, time and time again, Western after Western. The thought made her laugh, Kurt looked up sharply.

'What's the joke?' he asked. Her laughter had coincided with another hatchet job, so she hastily pointed out that she wasn't laughing at that, and tried to explain what she was laughing at. Kurt didn't seem to understand.

'Well they're actors,' he said. 'That's what they do. Anyway, I don't see why it's funny.'

'It's not funny.'

'Why did you laugh, then?'

She couldn't explain. Because it was ridiculous? Because it didn't make sense? Because...

'I don't know' she said. 'Why don't they get real Red Indians to play the parts?'

'Well, there aren't many of them,' he said. 'A lot of them died from diseases. And anyway they won't have their photos taken because they believe that the camera steals their souls, so I don't suppose they'd let people film them.'

'Oh,' she said and tried to watch the film. But she looked at the red men and saw white men underneath, and couldn't help feeling that they were trying to take her in, and that she'd blown their cover. She couldn't watch it any more, it had stopped making sense. She got up and went to make a coffee. After a few minutes Kurt appeared at the kitchen door.

'What's the matter, Honey,' he asked, 'Is it too violent?'

She remained silent for a moment, staring hard at the drops of coffee as they dripped through the filter into the jug, Drip, drip, drip, drip...

'Yes,' she said finally, her eyes still fixed on the jug, 'It's too violent.'

Although it was early, and she was half asleep, Marilyn

could tell something was wrong as soon as she stumbled into the living room. Breakfast TV was on, and her parents were watching it intently, their food untouched.

'What's up?' she asked, 'Is something wrong? Has something happened?'

No reply.

She turned her attention to the television.

'Reports are still soming in about last night's American bombing of Tripoli and Benghasi,' said the news reader. 'Numbers of dead and injured are not yet known, but unofficial figures put it at hundreds, maybe more. Amongst the injured are members of Colonel Quadaffi's family. The whereabouts of Quadaffi himself is not yet known.

The Prime Minister has been strongly criticised by the Opposition for permitting the F111 bombers to launch their attack on Libya from a US military base in Upper Heyford, Oxfordshire. Mr Kinnock described her actions as 'grossly irresponsible', and 'putting British Citizens in jeopardy.'

'Now over to John Dennis in Tripoli for an update on the situation.'

Shots were shown of the bombed streets of Tripoli. There were piles of rubble where houses had been, whole streets flattened by the strength of the blast.

Some shots were full of people rushing around, but in others there was nothing but the lifeless ruined buildings and a numb silence. In one of these shots a woman sat on the ground by what used to be a house, so still she could have been part of the rubble herself. She turned her head and her face looked directly out from the screen. Her expression was not one of sorrow or anger, but of a bland incomprehension, so intense that it hit Marilyn like a punch in the stomach.

Then came shots of crowds of young men in the street, shouting, crying, some of them waving guns, all of them looking angry, looking furious.

'The mood here is ugly,' said the reporter. 'Emotions are running high. There are mobs on the street chanting anti-British and anti-American slogans. They are screaming for vengeance. 'For every drop of Libyan blood spilled', they are howling, 'the people of Libya will spill ten drops of the blood of our aggressors.' It is certainly not a comfortable time to be a Briton in Libya.'

The news went on and on. There were condemnations of the acts of Reagan and Thatcher from other countries; retired military men commenting on the efficiency of the attack; and talk about the evacuation of Britons and Americans from Libya. But, most importantly, there was discussion of retaliation. Would Libya bomb Britain? And if so, would they use their nuclear capacity? This was debated for some time. An expert on Libyan affairs was interviewed. He said he had calculated that whilst there was only a 10% chance of nuclear attack; the likelihood of a non-nuclear reprisal was more like 50%. Even the newsreader seemed slightly shaken at this. The atmosphere of muffled panic which had prevailed throughout the reports suddenly became more evident. Then suddenly the programme ended, leaving Marilyn dazed, staring at the empty screen. Ceefax came on with 'The March of the Dambusters' blaring out cheerfully as background music. She turned the TV off.

Her parents had left for work and she hadn't even noticed. She should have been in work herself half an hour ago. She thought about going, but couldn't face it. It seemed almost trivial. She wandered around the house aimlessly, looking at things, picking them up and putting them back down. The tidy chaos seemed comforting, for once. It seemed fitting. Silly to pretend that order mattered in little ways, when you considered the total confusion of the real state of things.

She looked out of the window at the street. It was quiet, and looked as peaceful as it always did at this time of the day. But normally it looked solid, as if it had been there forever, and would always be there; now, however, it seemed fragile and impermanent. She could see it as piles of dust and rubble. The woman she could see in the house opposite would be dead, and so would the man pushing the pram down the street. And so would she.

She thought of the film of Tripoli she'd seen that morning. The destroyed streets; the chaos; the look on the woman's face. The look asked a question that was becoming more and more insistent in Marilyn's mind. It was the only thing that seemed worth thinking.

The question was 'Why?'

She went to work the next morning because she couldn't think of anything else to do. The supervisor gave her a verbal warning, but she'd reached a state of calmness (or was it numbness) where nothing made any impact on her.

She felt more distant than ever as she stood behind the counter that morning. In fact she felt disembodied. She floated slowly up towards the ceiling and watched her body, switched onto robot, serving up fast food and smiling.

Suddenly the doors were pushed open, forcefully, and Kurt exploded into the restaurant, looking worried and agitated.

'Marilyn!' he said. Reluctantly, she came down from the ceiling. 'Honey, where the Hell have you been? I was looking everywhere for you yesterday. Listen,' he went on, without giving her chance to answer, which was just as well because she didn't have an answer that would make sense to him, 'Listen, I have to talk to you. It's very important.'

'What's wrong?' she asked, trying to come out of her numbness and respond to his state of anxiety; and failing.

'I can't explain now,' he answered. 'I have to rush. I'll tell you later. It's ...' He kept running his fingers through his hair looking nervy and agitated. 'It's ... Hey, look, I'd better go. I'll pick you up after work.' He attempted a smile. 'Bye Honey', he said.

He had imposed a veneer of calmness over his anxiety by the time he met her after work, but she could tell that he was still nervous. And frightened. She'd never seen him look frightened before. He was always so confident.

They went to a pub they knew would be quiet. It was so quiet that there was only one other customer, a middle aged man slumped on a barstool, downing whiskies and trying to chat up the barmaid.

There was a sign on the bar annoucing that it was the Happy Hour.

They sat in an alcove and she waited for him to tell her his news.

Her state of numbness had prevented her from developing

any curiosity about the matter that was troubling him, although she knew it must be something important. She had developed a fatalistic attitude that was almost like armour. She felt that anything that happened would be all the same to her.

Kurt sat there, smoking nervously and staring hard into his drink. Then he took a large gulp of it and looked at her for a long time with a mixture of pain and regret in his expression.

Then he sighed, and said slowly, flatly 'I have to go home, Marilyn. The company are re-calling all American personnel working in Britain. It's ... it's not safe for me to be here.'

In the silence that followed she searched around for some sort of feeling, but the numbness had deepened into an emotional paralysis, and the only thing that was different was a sick feeling at the bottom of her stomach.

'When do you have to ...?'

'Tomorrow,' he said and looked at her with pity as much as sorrow. 'I don't want to go, Marilyn,' he said. 'I don't want to leave you.'

She suddenly said 'I love you, Kurt', but the words seemed so far away that she wondered if she'd imagined speaking them.

But when he said 'Oh, Marilyn,' and stroked her hair, his voice was shaky, so he must have heard her.

They went back to his flat, and she hardly recognised it. It was in total chaos. There were half-packed trunks and suitcases strewn around the rooms, and Kurt's belongings were piled in untidy heaps in corners, on the furniture, on the floor.

There was not a trace of the well ordered flat she knew. Its tidy harmony had vanished into disarray.

After a couple of drinks her anaesthetised emotions began to unfreeze a little. She thought of life without Kurt, and seemed dull and grey. She thought how his intense reality set him apart from other people; how everyone else seemed like shadows compared to him. She felt as if some of this reality had rubbed off onto her, making her more alive, too. And now he was going. She realised how flat and drab everything would be without him. Suddenly she couldn't bear it. Hiding her face in his shoulder she cried and cried until she was exhausted. He began to kiss her, and then slowly, blindly, they began to make love with a desperation that was almost violent, neither of them very aware of the other's presence, except as a body, obsessed, as each was with their own personal fear and loss.

It wasn't until his flight was nearly due at the airport that she realised she didn't even have a photograph of him.

He fumbled around in his flight bag muttering 'I know there's one in here somewhere,' and eventually handed her a snapshot.

'It's not a very good one' he said. It was taken against a background of trees and the vague patches of light and shade behind him made him seem brighter, sharper and more real than ever. But he'd held his smile for the camera, and the result was a grin that was almost manic.

It was still Kurt, though. She looked up from the image to the solid flesh and blood Kurt, and at that moment his flight was called.

'Don't forget me, Kurt', she said as he melted away into the crowd of people hurrying to board their plane.

As she walked down the street to Jo's house, Marilyn thought about the letter. Although it had arrived three days ago she hadn't told anyone about it yet, not even Jo, who had shared all her secrets, ever since that fateful day when they had crossed the threshold of St Joseph's Mixed Infants together, and Jo had managed to get them both into trouble within an hour of being there. Since they had left school, Marilyn hadn't seen that much of her though. She'd moved around the country a lot, living in squats, or peace camps, or on the road. She'd recently come back to stay with her family for a few weeks before carrying out her grand plan of hitching round Europe.

It was Jo who had helped Marilyn through the first few weeks of Kurt's absence, feeding her sufficient alcohol and dope to ease the pain and dragging her out when she tried to spend evenings in her room staring at his picture.

Should she tell Jo about Kurt's letter? Jo had never met

Kurt, and when Marilyn had showed her his picture she had laughed and said 'It looks as if he's wearing Mickey Mouse ears.' And it was true that if you looked at the photograph in a certain way, the shade behind his head did look a bit like that, but Marilyn had never noticed it before. It spoiled the photograph for her now.

Was she going to tell her? What would Jo's reaction be if she told her Kurt had asked her to marry him and go and live in California. And become, as he put it, a 'Fully fledged citizen of the good old US of A'. She didn't know. She didn't even know what her own reaction was. It seemed so perfect — living in America, married to Kurt. No more grey skies, no more Dreamburger Company. She didn't know why she was so confused about it, why she didn't write back at once with a resounding 'Yes'.

She pushed open the door of Jo's house and shouted 'Jo! It's me!' One of her sisters called back 'She's outside, Lyn.'

Marilyn went round to the back of the house where Jo was helping her mother peg clothes on the line.

'Hello love,' said Mrs Moran. 'I haven't seen you for a while. How's everyone?'

'Fine', said Marilyn.

'And Frances?'

Frances, Marilyn's oldest sister had just had her fourth baby, bringing the headcount of Marilyn's nephews and nieces up to ten. 'She's better now. The doctors gave her some tablets that stopped her being depressed.'

'That's good,' said Mrs Moran, and was about to continue when a shrill voice from the house cried out.

'Mum, Paul's eating a spider,' and she sighed and handed the laundry basket to Marilyn.

'He's only just had his breakfast', she said, and went in to investigate.

The two girls chatted as they pegged out the line of clothes.

'I'm going next week', said Jo.

'That's soon', Marilyn said, trying not to sound downcast.

'Cheer up, Lyn,' said Jo and put her arm around her. 'I'll send you postcards from everywhere I go.'

'Yeah,' said Marilyn 'I'll think of you lazing around in the sun while I'm slaving away in the Dreamburger Company, you lucky cow.'

Jo looked at her thoughtfully for a few seconds. 'You don't have to stay', she said.

Marilyn looked at her in surprise thinking that somehow she'd guessed the contents of Kurt's letter. But no. She couldn't have.

What did she mean, then?

'You could always come with me', Jo said.

'What? Me!' exclaimed Marilyn. 'Me hitch round Europe! You've got to be joking!'

'Why not?' asked Jo.

'Well, it's ... well I ... I haven't got any money for one thing.'

'I'm taking a hundred quid. That's all you'd need.'

'Well, I've got my holiday pay to come. But ...'

'But nothing! It'll be easy. We can go down to Greece and get some work in a bar. And then later on there's fruit picking. There's nothing to be worried about, people do it all the time. And anyway,' she added 'we can always sell our passports if we get desperate.'

Marilyn looked horrified. 'You'll end up in jail, Josephine Moran', she said. 'I think I should come with you to keep you out of trouble.'

Jo laughed. 'You're coming then?' she asked.

Marilyn thought about Kurt, but she could only remember him the way he was in the photo, with the manic grin and the Mickey Mouse ears, and it all seemed far away, somehow, like a film she'd seen a long time ago.

'Well?' asked Jo. 'Are you coming?'

'Perhaps,' said Marilyn, 'perhaps I will.'

Daddy's Toy

Olivia Michael

Sandy had always been daddy's little girl, as long as she could remember. She always waited in great excitement for him to come home, and would always do whatever he said, though she frequently disobeyed her mother.

'You're your daddy's girl alright,' her mother would occasionally grumble.

Whenever the three of them were together, Sandy would sit closest to her father and hold his hand. Sometimes her mother would look hurt and say, 'She doesn't love me like she loves you, Brian,' and Sandy would run to her mother crying, 'It's not true!', burying her face in her mother's skirts because she knew, really, that it was.

Sandy lived with her mummy and daddy in a maisonette on a new council estate. Mummy was happier there since this estate was not as rough as the old one, and their home was like a proper house, built on top of a flat and connected to all the others by a long balcony. Daddy worked in a builder's yard nearby. Sometimes Sandy could peek through the fence and watch him work. Mummy was often out at nights selling things for her 'club', make-up or jewellery. When daddy looked after Sandy he would play games with her in which he was a monster and she had to run and hide. When he found her, he would rush towards her, growling horribly as Sandy screamed. And he would toss her into the air, then pin her down over his knee, pull her pants down and smack her bare bottom. Sandy was not sure whether this was part of the game or not, though daddy pretended it was. He never played in this way when mummy was in the room. And sometimes he would touch her in a way which sent strange new sensations quivering down the lower part of her body. Confused, excited and nervous all at once, she would run to her mummy if she was nearby, or if not, stay where he held her, with a pink and bursting face.

'You mustn't tell your mother,' daddy would warn, stroking softly. 'She wouldn't understand — mummies don't. She might get upset. Then *anything* could happen,' he would finish, with menacing emphasis. Vague imaginings filled Sandy's mind with dread. When he finished daddy would always say 'You love your daddy don't you?' and Sandy would always nod, clinging to him. So whenever she went near her mother she would hover around anxiously and aimlessly, until her mother would exclaim 'For heaven's sake Sandy! What's to do? Go to your father!'

Sometimes daddy liked to play with her when mummy was in the same room, but with her back to them. Daddy's fingers would lift the back of her skirt and slip inside her knickers. At these times daddy would get very excited, swallowing repeatedly and pressing Sandy's hand to the front of his trousers, where the bulge was big and hard. Sandy felt his excitement, compounded by a terrible fear, in case her mother turned round and caught them. Forbidden feelings caused her legs to tremble.

Daddy quarrelled more and more often with mummy. Sandy would listen on the stairs, digging her fingernails into her cheeks, and eventually bursting into great, tearing sobs, which usually they did not hear. She was terrified that one day, when daddy got angry, he would tell mummy about their games, and the terrible 'something' of her imaginings would happen. So often when daddy was in a bad mood, Sandy would try to distract him. All she had to do was to press herself up against him and kiss him in the way he liked, full on the mouth, opening her lips for his big, wet tongue. And with a grunt of pleasure, he would pull her onto his knee and slip his fingers between her legs.

It became harder to be with mummy, and Sandy began to avoid her. Inwardly she began to be convinced that mummy could tell her dreadful secret just from looking at her in the mysterious way that mummies sometimes can. She tried hard not to let her mother look at her at all, and her mother complained all the more that Sandy only wanted her father, she was her daddy's little girl. But Sandy did not want to play with her father any more either. By 'play', he always meant the same game. And she had soon learned that it was daddy's game, and he made all the rules. The first night he tried to put his thing inside her, Sandy screamed, and then had one of her asthma attacks. Mummy had been out, but daddy had sent for the doctor, and eventually Sandy had calmed down. But daddy had tried again the next night, and the next. 'Take it easy, girl, take it easy,' he said softly, as she squirmed. 'I don't want to hurt you.' After he finished, he smoothed the tears from her cheeks and stroked her hair. 'Ssh lass,' he would say, until she quietened down. And soon she could accommodate him without much discomfort. And it was alright. Daddy loved her. He kissed her as he tucked her in at night, whilst repeating that she mustn't ever tell mummy. Sandy underststood that. If mummy found out she would not want to know Sandy any more. She would hate her. Sandy's mind bounced away from this dreadful prospect like a ball.

One day, when Sandy got up, she could not find her mother. The previous night she had listened to her parents quarrelling for hours, rocking backwards and forwards on the top step of the stairs and moaning unconsciously. Eventually she must have fallen asleep and been carried into bed.

But now it was morning, and mummy was not there. Swallowing her fear, Sandy faced her father. 'Where's me mum?' she asked, apprehensively. Daddy's newspaper scarcely twitched.

'She's at Aunty Vi's,' he said. 'She'll be back soon. You'd best get off to school.'

After school, Sandy ran all the way home, but the house was empty. Daddy came home early and let them both in. He was glum and uncommunicative. He did not want to play, or answer questions. Sandy went to bed with a dull ache in her stomach. She could not sleep and, much later, heard daddy going to bed. He did not call in to say goodnight. Sandy's desolation was complete.

Mummy did not come home the next day either. In the evening daddy took Sandy round to Aunty Vi's to see if he could speak to her. 'She's not here,' said Aunty Vi, folding stout arms across her breasts. Daddy did not believe this at first, and he quarrelled with Aunty Vi, but eventually she convinced him that mummy had indeed moved on — somewhere up north — she didn't know where — to stay with friends. Sandy and daddy trudged home in silence. With her hand in his, Sandy could sense her father's black, unspoken anger, and this, together with her awful suspicions as to the cause of her mother's departure, left her feeling crushed and numb. She undressed and lay in bed like a stone.

The next afternoon, as Sandy sat on the doorstep of her house, daddy approached, looking weary and dispirited. He said, 'Hello princess,' as he let them both in, but Sandy could not smile. The hollow fear which had begun when her mother had left still gripped her inwardly. Inside, daddy switched the lights on and put the kettle on the stove. Then he sat down and drew Sandy towards him. 'I've got something for you,' he said, and smiled wanly. Into her hand he pressed a key. Daddy said she was a big girl now, seven years old, nearly eight. She could let herself in after school. Daddy could trust her not to touch anything she shouldn't or do anything silly. Sandy knew that this meant that he didn't expect her mummy to return. With tears stinging her eyes she turned from him and hauled herself heavily up the stairs. Pausing at the door of her mother's bedroom, she again experienced a sensation of absolute unreality. She could not accept what was happening to her. Most of her mother's things were still there. The wardrobe door hung open and mummy's clothes bulged from it. The dressing table was still littered with perfume and make-up. Wearily, Sandy went to her own room and climbed into her crumpled bed. Cold tears ran noiselessly down her face. Her mother had found out about Sandy. She would never want to see her again.

Sandy's bedroom door clicked unexpectedly, and Sandy's heart leapt. Daddy entered, saying 'Sandy?' quietly, and sat down on her bed. He began to touch her hair and face. Soon he shifted himself so that his whole body was on top of hers. Sandy lay like a rag doll beneath him. She did not want to say the dirty words he normally liked her to say. Soon he began to moan, then, unexpectedly, burst into tears. He buried his face against her neck and sobbed.

'She'll not come back, Sandy — she's never coming back,' he got out eventually. Sandy cried too, her arms around his neck. At length they fell asleep together in the little bed.

The next day in school, Sandy had an idea which lit up her whole afternoon, so that she could hardly wait to get home. She let herself in and rushed upstairs to her mother's room. Pulling off her skirt and jersey, she rummaged through her mother's wardrobe. Eventually she selected a cream satin blouse, one of her mother's best, a navy, pleated skirt, cream high-heeled shoes, and a long string of fake pearls. Sandy had watched her mother dress many times. Copying her from memory, she arranged the clothes on the bed and, before dressing, went to the dressing table. She smudged on bright blue eyeshadow and pale orange lipstick, then sprayed herself liberally with perfume. Next she dressed, bunching up the skirt at the waist to stop it falling down. Looking at herself in the mirror, Sandy felt pleased with the results of her experiment. Daddy had often said how much she looked like her mother. Now he would be surprised at how much like her she could be. She clopped downstairs precariously in the large shoes, to the kitchen. Sandy wished she could prepare tea for when her father came in, as mummy always did, but she was not allowed to touch the cooker. So she sat down on the kitchen stairs and waited.

Daddy did not come home. Sandy waited on the stairs until well past dark, then made herself some bread and cheese. She prowled anxiously around, then tried to read. Suffocated by fear, she could not concentrate. Suppose daddy, like mummy, never came home? After interminable hours, Sandy heard voices outside the door. Leaping up, she ran quickly forwards, rubbing her face which was all smudged from crying. Laughing loudly, her father let himself in, unsteadily, and paused in surprise as he saw Sandy.

'Well, I don't know!' he exclaimed, with another great laugh. 'Look at this, Sal!' Sandy stared as the pink, giggling face of a young woman appeared behind her father. She followed him in, wriggling her plump shoulders as she removed her coat.

'You look like Miss World, luv,' she giggled, as daddy turned Sandy round. They both admired her, turning her this
way and that.

'But you shouldn't be up at this time, Miss,' daddy observ-
ed. 'You'd best get off to bed now, this minute!' and with
a spank he sent her off in the direction of her bedroom.

The sound of laughter faded as the door closed behind
Sandy, and she advanced into darkness. In the empty hall,
with the uncarpeted floor, her big shoes made a 'clop-clop-
clopping' noise, which echoed in the silence.

Still life

Liz Tolan

Mabel returned home with her shopping in a chequered trolley, the chop on top so as not to get squashed. As she walked up the path she noticed Arthur in his garden next door, painting things white. He had finished the edges of the steps and was working his way along the low dry-stone wall which enclosed a bed of dwarf subjects.

'Good afternoon,' she called, over the privet.

'Oh, hello Mabel,' said Arthur, straightening up and sprinkling white specks onto the lawn. 'Didn't see you there.'

Mabel leant the trolley against the door and took her key out of her handbag.

'Here,' said Arthur, 'I've plenty of paint here, do you want anything touching up?'

'No, thank you,' replied Mabel, 'not just at the moment.'

'It's no trouble, you know,' continued Arthur. 'I like to keep busy. And the paint was on special offer — two for the price of one — Brilliant White.'

'Thank you,' said Mabel, 'but there's nothing I need painting just now.'

She unlocked the door and went inside.

'You only have to say the word,' Arthur was saying.

The house was silent, held in suspension since the morning when Mabel had left for the 8.15 bus. In the hall motes of dust hung in the dim beam of light from the transom window. Mabel went into the kitchen with her trolley. It was Thursday; half day closing at the city centre store where she worked in the Toy Department. After finishing work she had eaten lunch in a nearby cafe and had then walked to the supermarket where she did her weekly shop. She had come home on the bus; the conductor had helped with the trolley.

Mabel switched on the wireless, tuned to Radio Four. The play was about to begin. A small mirror, used for checking her appearance before answering the door, hung on the kitchen wall, and as she passed back and forth, unpacking the shopping and filing it away in cupboard, fridge, vegetable rack and bread bin, she caught glimpses of her face, disembodied. When everything was put away she filled the kettle and put it on to boil. The chop was left on the worktop in its polythene wrapping.

When she rinsed out her teacup in the sink Mabel saw Arthur, in his back garden now, painting the clothes post. In her own garden blue tits were swinging from the half coconut which hung from a branch of the Copper Beech. Later, as she prepared the vegetables to accompany her chop, she saw that Arthur had painted the rustic bird table which he had erected the previous summer. It stood like a lighthouse in the grey March afternoon.

That evening Mabel watched snooker on the television until after midnight. When she went upstairs she looked out at the familiar silhouette of her garden, still and silent, before drawing the curtains and climbing into her bed under the faded eiderdown.

On Friday morning Mabel bumped into Betty Binns as she hurried to catch the 8.15 bus. Betty was walking her Yorkshire Terrier.

'You haven't met my Midgy, have you,' she asked, picking up the animal to introduce it.

Mabel missed the 8.15 and arrived at work too late to comb her hair and freshen her lipstick.

The other assistants in the Toy Department were considerably younger than she. Beverly was eighteen and Susan was twenty three. Mrs. Hardwick, who worked three mornings a week, was the mother of school children. Beverly's hair had developed a green streak overnight. Mabel didn't say anything but Mr. Mortimer did when he did his rounds.

At lunchtime Mabel took her sandwiches and flask to the canteen. She sat with Doreen from Hosiery who had joined the firm at the same time as she had. Doreen had an enormous bosom which was a constant source of interest; it brimmed rudely over the V neck of her regulation sweater. She had full lips which seemed constantly in motion either eating or speaking. She talked loudly and without prompting about her husband, Ted, their children, Samantha, Karen, and Craig, her two Siamese cats, her last year's holiday, and her mother's operation.

After lunch they went to the staff rest room and did their faces and hair, monitoring the results in the large mirror over the washbasins. Doreen's reflection wore red lips and large, clip-on earrings; Mabel's had pink lips and pale spectacles.

It was still light when Mabel got off the bus that evening. Boys were kicking a ball across the street and back; two girls roller-skated past her gate. Next door the standard lamp was lit in Arthur and Anne's sitting room and the curtains were still drawn back. Mabel could see Arthur watching the news.

A piece of haddock was waiting in the fridge for Mabel. She cooked mashed potato and frozen runner beans to go with it and had an individual mousse as dessert. In the evening she wrote a letter to her cousin who lived by the sea and afterwards read some of her library book. Later on there was snooker again and she watched that before going to bed with a warm drink. It was a moonlit night. When she checked the view from the bedroom window, she saw clothes post and bird table shining in the garden next door, but her own shrubs and trees were quiet and still.

Mabel had to work one Saturday in four at the Toy Department. When she worked the Saturday she would have a day off during the following week. This Saturday she was working. The other assistants were usually part-time, Saturday-only staff. Today one of them was ill so Graham, the youth from Domestic Appliances, had been brought in to help. Graham suffered from adolescent acne but was very capable with electronic games and anything requiring batteries. He was happy to explain to Mabel the workings of the latest gadget.

Halfway through the morning, when the department was getting quite busy, a young woman with a child in a pushchair and another clinging to her arm approached Mabel and thrust a grubby package into her hand.

'I want something done about this,' she announced.

Mabel opened the crumpled brown paper bag and took out a boxed board game.

'Two of the mice are missing and the flip-a-dice doesn't work,' said the woman.

Mabel pointed out that the game looked well used and asked if she had a receipt.

'No, our Billy must have got hold of it. Billy!'

The child had let go of his mother's sleeve and was sitting astride a tricycle aimed at a display of jigsaw puzzles. Mabel explained that nothing could be done without proof of purchase at which the woman began to shout and gesticulate making other shoppers turn and stare. Mabel had to send Graham to fetch Mr. Mortimer who quickly came and led the woman and her pushchair to his office. Billy followed trailing.

Doreen's Saturday shift did not coincide with hers so at lunchtime Mabel slipped out to post her letter. She needed to buy a stamp and there were long queues at the Post Office. An obnoxious smelling tramp was annoying everyone, shambling from queue to queue muttering obscenities. Outside, the pedestrian precinct was busy with shoppers and groups of strangely dressed youths. At intervals people stood selling flags in aid of charity. One enthusiastic volunteer stuck one on Mabel's lapel and she had to stop and search in her purse for an appropriate coin to put in the tin. Further along, young people were handing leaflets to passersby. Someone was playing the guitar on a corner and two men were selling Gent's Hankies from a case on the ground. It was difficult to make headway through the crowds. When she got back to the store Mabel had only just time to eat her sandwiches and drink a cup of tea from her flask before going back on duty.

The bus home was less busy than during the week. When Mabel got in she switched on the immersion heater before preparing her meal and, after she had eaten and washed the dishes, went for a long soak in the bath. She could hear children shouting in the street outside although it was dark. While she was powdering herself, the phone rang and she hurried downstairs in her dressing-gown to answer it.

'Is Adrian in?' asked a high pitched female voice.

During the evening Mabel fell asleep on the sofa and woke later to find the television buzzing, all programmes having finished. She went into the kitchen and made herself a cup of tea and buttered some cream crackers. Through the gap in the kitchen curtains she could see the outlines of the neighbouring houses, all in darkness. Behind her own reflection, the shaft of light from the kitchen illuminated the waiting grass. Mabel took her tray upstairs and drew the bedroom curtains quickly without looking out. She read a few pages of her book while eating her supper, then turned out the light and slept, restlessly. The travelling alarm ticked softly.

On Sunday morning Mabel went downstairs in her dressing gown and put on the kettle. Passing the kitchen mirror, she caught sight of a face. She took the mirror down and put it in the cutlery drawer. Then she went to the cupboard under the stairs and pulled out cardboard boxes and carrier bags of cleaning equipment and discarded household items. The kettle whistled as she sorted through the jumble. She emerged with a tin of paint labelled Blush Pink, the shade of the bathroom. She went back into the kitchen, turned off the kettle, and took a knife from the drawer to prise open the lid. She stirred the crusted paint with the knife then returned to the cupboard for a paintbrush and went outside.

Arthur, standing in the bay window with the Sunday Express, said to Anne,

'Mabel's gone a bit bold all of a sudden. She's painting the door pink.'

'Pink?' said Anne. 'What, the front door?'

'Yes,' said Arthur.

Anne joined him at the window. 'Pink isn't a proper colour for a front door. Not to my mind.'

'Could be an undercoat, I suppose,' said Arthur.

'And she's still in her dressing gown,' said Anne.

'I offered her the Brilliant White only the other day,' said Arthur.

'She walked right past me on Tuesday,' said Anne.

'I would have done it for her, she only had to say the word,' said Arthur.

'Let's hope it is an undercoat. Pink isn't right at all. It'll make the whole street look odd,' said Anne.

'Well, there's nowt so queer as folk, as my old Dad used to say,' said Arthur, moving over to the armchair and opening his paper.

Anne plumped the cushions on the settee then left the room.

Mabel continued to paint, specks of Blush Pink spattering the doorstep, her slippers, and her candlewick dressing gown.

News Item: Woman Re-united with Virginity

Dorothy Byrne

An overjoyed Burnage woman paid tribute last night to the sharp-eyed pensioner who found her lost virginity.

Elizabeth Stewart, 23, of Moor Crescent, was broken-hearted when she realised she'd mislaid her virginity in the city centre yesterday morning.

'I didn't notice it was gone till I got home. I rang the shops I'd been in and contacted the police, but it was no good. I just burst into tears,' she said.

But 79-year-old Mabel Granger, a grandmother of seven from Devonshire Road, Longsight, had spotted Elizabeth's virginity lying on the food counter in Woolworths.

'At first I didn't know what it was,' Mabel explained, 'but I decided to take it to the police station because I was brought up to be honest.'

Police contacted Elizabeth who rushed to the city office to find her virginity intact.

'It hadn't been damaged at all, I am so pleased. There are no words to express how grateful I am to Mrs Granger and this will teach me not to be so forgetful, I must have put it down while I was buying some cheese.'

A police spokesman added: 'This is actually quite a common occurence but it's rare for a woman to reclaim her virginity. Normally we auction them off after six months and give the money to charity.'

An Unextraordinary Day

Joan Batchelor

...the drapes glided silently aside as she moved out into the sudden dazzle of a million multi coloured lights and the deafening applause ... they loved her ... the soft leather of her costume stroked her thighs to a building ecstacy as she raised her arms. There was an adoring silence, a living expectancy. She licked her peppermint tasting lips as she gave a sideways glance to the drummer in his tiger-skin pants that strained at the crotch without distracting her million writhing fans now sobbing her name as they stretched silver tipped fingers towards her electrically charged body which dominated the stage. There was a staccato that lifted her mind high and the drummer leaned forward with an animal yell...

'Damn that clock!' Her dream exploded with a shower of rainbows. Sue groaned, unwilling to give up the adoration of a million for the bad temper of her young son. The radio alarm throbbed to the latest pop sensation of the moment and she curled a lip. She allowed her mind to open slowly first, keeping her eyes shuttightly. The staccato of high heels drummed above her head in the flat above. Why didn't they cover the bloody bare boards? if not carpet then clothing, rags, sacks ... newspapers. Slowly now ... wake happy.

Birds gave out little disgruntled cheeps of sheer unhappiness. The muted traffic snarled. The sky wept tired droplets onto the dirt encrusted windows. Sue moved an impatient hand to cut off the mindless, magpie chatter of the disc jockey who seemed hell bent on wickedly waking a trembling world to yet another day of rank debauchery amongst the supermarket vegetables and blood lust over the butchers counter. Doors slammed. Cars started up. Babies wailed … but not hers … her teenage son was sound asleep amongst the squalor of rancid socks and hurled about clothes. Singles littered his boy-sized pool table and LPs were there to grind underfoot. She kept her eyes screwed shut. Allowing feeling to seep into her rag doll limp body. The sheets were warm beneath her body yet cold where the duvet had dragged onto the floor. She felt about for the knickers which she had kicked off in the heat of the night before and dragged them on beneath her short cotton nightie. A book slithered to the floor. At last she parted her reluctant eyelids … waking with a sudden determination and energy. She sat up in the rumpledbed and met the eyes of the tousled head framed in the mirror opposite, Ugh … she averted her eyes hastily and scanned them instead over the papers tottering at the brink of her overloaded desk. On the back of her chair her black lace bra was lovingly entwined with her patched jeans … make up was strewn about her dressing table higgledy-piggledy. She glanced at the clock and swung her long legs out of the bed cracking her knees on the floor. Christ … when would she remember that her bed as yet was a mattress on the floor…

Rubbing her bruised knees, her eyes smarting with tiredness and pain, she pummelled the wall that separated her bedroom from her son's….

'Get up … damn you.' she yelled, and stubbed her toe for being such a crotchetty bitch….

'I'm up … I'm up…' returned a voice that leapt from bass to falsetto on the repeat.

She gathered up the mail and staggered back to bed grabbing her glasses on the way…. One bill, one bank statement enclosing a threatening letter, and one calendar of events for the following month from a local writers workshop … the bank statement and letter followed the calendar into the overflowing bin. She put on her glasses and the bill swam into focus. She stuffed it into the unpaid bills section with a grim smile….

There was an outburst of Madness — the pop group —

which assailed her ear drums but she winced bravely and scrambled back by the door groping around the garbage bag her son had failed to remove and finding yet another letter and a cheque for £5 from the courts, maintenance towards the upkeep of her 13 year old son. She clambered back into bed, dislodging her knitting and her breath freshener from beneath her pillows then sat crosslegged in the centre-pit of her mattress listening to the thumps and crashes that told her that her son, affectionately known as Jonah, was by now back in the land of the living and wreaking vengeance upon his furniture, swearing as he trampled his LPs into the carpet. . . .

'Where's my clean socks? . . . there's no socks.' he yelled. 'I can't find my pen.. have you had my red pen? Have you ironed a shirt? I can't find a shirt. . . .'

She opened her letter as she let him rant. He grunted as he found missing articles, swore as he fell over mounds of untidiness in his room . . . he would learn the hard way. He splashed water in the bathroom, spread cornflakes over the kitchen floor then he walked over them. He burst into her bedroom shouting 'knock-knock. . .' She sat on unperturbed, he flung himself into her swivel chair and swung as he stuffed cornflakes into his mouth . . . she glanced up, her glasses on her nose.

His black hair stood up on the crown of his head. Down grew very softly over his pubescent cheeks. A spot glared from his chin. His navy uniform was neat, his white shirt unbuttoned at the neck to show off a short rope of small white shells about a slightly grubby neck.

'He's sent another letter. . .' he acknowledged it with a gesture of his spoon, then beat at a cornflake that dropped onto his dark trousers. She grimaced ruefully as she set the letter aside and took stock of her son. His dark eyes met her own.

'Next time you wash before you put a shirt on. . .' she said without hope in her voice.

'You wanna coffee?' He grinned, ignoring the demand but with a lift to his eyebrow that showed he had heard. He barged out and crashed around the kitchen then banged an uncompromising concoction by the side of the bed and held out a hand. . . .

'You need milk and a paper . . .' she fumbled for her purse beneath her pillow . . . he tripped over the mat and hurtled out as she sipped the bitter brew. Addict; she thought; her eyes on the dinky-toy traffic far beneath her high rise flat.The shrill of children's voices rose with a gathering frequency. Her son tore back and threw the milk and paper on her bed. She held out her hand for the change. He grinned as he dug into his pocket.

'I'm off . . . 'byeeee'. He departed in a whoosh that left the flat aching with the sudden silence. She sat very still drinking the rest of her coffee.

Outside sounds faded as the flats about her woke with a groan, a laugh, shout, hoover, radio, scram, footsteps, hammering . . . one great digestive tract, lungs and heart and all contained within four walls. A whole nervous system. Arteries.

She got out of bed and carefully tidied it, placing the teddy bear called Edward McGregor and her half read book on top. She dressed then moved through the rooms like a virago, mercilessly putting them to order, tidying, polishing, sweeping, and mopping. She washed up and left the dishes to drain then filled the laundry bag with reeking socks, panties, tee shirts, jeans, towels and sheets. Then she sat at her desk and made out the household accounts for the next month very carefully and a list of chores for the day, each to be ticked off in red when completed. She was a fervent list maker . . . some order in a chaotic life.

In the bathroom she bathed, examining her breasts for lumps as part of her morning toilette, as she would clean her teeth, cream her face and make-up her eyes. All in order. She bared her teeth as she scooped his hair out of the plug hole and wiped up soap and grubby finger marks along the bath. Ugh.

Back at her desk she put on her glasses and picked up his letter. Divorced from her for over a year he still failed to adjust. She frowned with irritation. Well worn phrases flashed before her eyes. They had become more habit, his letters were always the same, beginning with love and carrying through agony into hatred, then his gross sexual fantasies taking over and erupting his neat forward sloping handwriting into a blue inked scrawl of drunken heavings. Once she would have cried with the horrific pity of it all ... now ... well, she couldn't let a letter destroy her winning struggle for survival. Really it was very simple. It had been a choice of drink or her and he chose. The drink won. Finis.

She walked into the kitchen where her son's bike lay on its back with inner tubes disgorged and awaiting attention. Reminding her that her smear test was due ... the River Irwell seeped sulkily past beneath the window carrying a thick layer of foam that had spewed from one of the many factories along its banks. She heaved up the basket of ironing to the table and wrestled to open the ironing board. Then she put eggs to boil as the iron heated and searched for a vegetable knife without luck....

She scrubbed new potatoes with the nail brush and put them to boil in their cleaned jackets. The iron spat so she ran it over the creased clothes watching them smooth with a pleasure that was sensual. She rescued the eggs and put the cooked potatoes onto a plate she rubbed off the skin ... then she put away the ironed garments and the ironing board before gathering peppers and a big bowlful of salad stuff together. She took her time making two plate salads and put them into the cool of the fridge. Then she made ice lollies and put them in the freezer. She washed up and cleaned all work surfaces of peels, pips, rind and shells until they gleamed. Then she changed the bin bag. It was all done bar the shopping and washing.

She put on a recorded tape of pop songs she had recorded from Franks records and sat to make out a shopping list., It was 1pm. The shops were shut until gone two so she glanced at the paper to see if there was anything of interest happening outside and then picked up her knitting and settled down for thirty minutes with a decent cup of coffee by her chair.

When she went back into the kitchen the shells and pips had clogged the sink so she opened the tool drawer with a reluctant sigh. She unblocked it in minutes and then poured down disinfectant ... she washed her hands, put on a jacket, grabbed her bag and purse, checked her keys and after a quick look round the flat left for the market.

She walked with sure steps to the stalls to buy what she had listed. Her purchases were made in very little time so she browsed through second hand books and considered having a coffee but was reluctant to pay the price listed so she lugged her bag home and made a mug there, putting away her groceries as she sipped it. It was time to write letters. So she sat at her desk and typed with her quick two finger work dashing straight to post them and dragging the garbage bag down with her in the lift, Jonah's job but still ... it was beginning to smell a bit ripe. Her plants looked a bit jaded so she fed them Baby Bio and talked to them softly. They perked up.

She ate her salad as she read. She had over 500 books and one third unread, a big pleasure to look forward to for dark winter evenings. Frank was coming tonight. She would colour shampoo her hair while Jonah ate his salad, and while she sat in the bath. Then she would change into something more suitable to a beer in the local than an elbow fight in the supermarket.

Her plate washed and she stretched her cramped limbs as a knock sounded at the door. She walked stiffly up the passage. Her grown up daughter stood there with harrassed face, her baby asleep in the trolley before her ... Sue felt her own face light up....

'Oh God she's been sick ... gallons of it...' Sue looked at he baby's glowing cheeks and peaceful posture ... she ushered her daughter in before her. She made coffee and offered it as the little girl woke with a big beam.

'The sod ... she always makes me look a liar...' grinned her mother. Apologetically the baby smiled then opened her mouth and vomited a vile mess over Sue's carpet ... she dived for paper towels then whisked the child out of her trolley and held her forward. The child was red hot.

'It's alright, just that bit of virus going around...' she soothed. Her daughter was even more alarmed....

'That virus that is killing kids all over the damned country ... don't say that, mam'

'Look darling, she looks far too well for that ... it's her

teeth and the heat, also a bit of a tummy bug I should think ... take her to the doctor when you get back so he can put your mind at rest....'

The baby played on the floor as they talked. She laughed and chortled, showing off her latest tooth and periodically throwing up over herself and whoever was closest at the time ... they sponged her down and made a fuss of her ... then it was a rush of gathering together teething gel, nappies, drinking mug, dummy, and bits and pieces before they departed in a flurry of hugs, kisses, baby waves and vomit.

Sue had just tidied up and washed when the door knocker sounded yet again. She dragged herself to the door ... Jonah stood there grinning....

'Where's your key?' she asked grimly.

'In my pocket...' he replied. She gave up. She plonked his salad onto the table ... where had the day fled? she still had to bath and colour shampoo her hair.

'Go to the launderette?' he asked.

'No.'

'I've no clean socks...' he moaned.

'Wash some, sunshine...' she ground out.

'It's not MY job...' he yelled. She bit her tongue and washed a pair by hand then put them into the cabinet to dry.

He departed in a whirr of bike leaving the television on, his bedroom lamp on, his light, the hall light, the bathroom light, his stereo, water puddled the kitchen floor, tools spread, uniform hurled over his pool table, toilet unflushed, lettuce and cucumber on plate, crumbs on floor, squash tipped and glass half full still, books on chairs, shoes in the hall, coat on the living room floor.

'Where are you going?' she yelled at his back.

'Off out...' he yelled back.

Her hair would have to wait. She began to look forward to a cool beer at the local.

A Pair of Jeans

Qaisra Shahraz

Miriam slid off the bus seat and glanced quickly at her watch. It was nearly 8 o'clock. Very late. Murmuring her goodbye to her two college friends, she made her way to the bus door and waited for her bus stop to approach. Once there she got off the bus and waved goodbye to her friends again. She pulled the jacket close to her body, becoming self-conscious about her jean-clad legs and the short jacket she wore at the top. All of a sudden she felt odd in her clothing. Yet they were just the type of clothes she needed to wear today; they were very appropriate for hill walking in the peak district. Somehow here, however, in the vicinity of her home she felt different. As she crossed the road and neared her own street, she was very conscious of her appearance and hoped that she would not meet anyone she knew.

Her mind turned to the day's outing. It had been a wonderful day. She was tired after climbing all those hills, but it was worth it. She felt exhilarated. She would welcome such an outing in the future. Remembering the time she hastened her pace. It was later than she anticipated. All of a sudden she remembered the phone call of yesterday evening. They said they were coming today. What if they had already arrived. She looked down at herself; at her legs. As soon as she got home she must discreetly make her way to her room and get changed.

Just as Miriam reached the gate of their semi-detached house, she heard a car pull up behind her. She turned around to see who it was. On seeing the colour of the car and the face behind the wheel her step faltered. Her face paled slightly. On pretence of opening the gate she turned round to collect her wits about her. Too late! They were already here. Her heart began to rock madly against her chest. Her clothes burned her. She wanted to quickly rush inside her home and peel them off.

She braced her shoulders. That was not the ways things were done, no matter what the circumstances. She turned round to greet the two people who had by now stepped out of the car, and were surveying her on the footpath. The woman was her future mother- in-law, a slightly frail woman dressed in shalwar and kameze with a chadar around her shoulders. The elderly man, behind the wheel earlier, was the woman's husband. He seemed to tower behind his wife.

Miriam found herself unable to look either of them in the eye. A watery hesitant smile played around her mouth. She did not know what to do, or how to act. Her usual vibrant self had disappeared. Her poise was lost. And yet these were the people she was supposed to impress. All she was aware of was the surreptitious glances they darted at her. In fact not at her, as Miriam, but at the figure, the appearance she presented clad in a pair of Levis and a skimpy leather jacket to top it up. This was not the Miriam they knew. This was a stranger, a western version of Miriam. She sensed their awkwardness. They too felt strange and did not know what to do with themselves. The father-in-law in particular avoided meeting her eye. He was looking somewhere else above her head.

He opened the gate and in two strides had crossed the driveway and was now knocking on the door of Miriam's home. Miriam stepped aside to let her future mother-in-law pass, who silently walked behind her husband. Miriam followed them as if in a daze. As she closed the gate behind her, she remembered that while the woman had accepted her mumbled greeting, by her reply 'wa lakum Assalam', the father-in-law, Miriam realised with mortification, had not paid much heed to her greeting, let alone responded to it. That was so uncharacteristic of him.

Miriam's mother, Fatima, opened the door to her guests. She beamed in pleasure as she beheld them. She had not expected Miriam to come with them, however. When she noticed her daughter tagging behind the two visitors, Fatima received a shock. Never before in her life had Miriam witnessed such a dramatic change in her mother's facial expression as the one that took place on her face when she saw her daughter. Normally she wouldn't have batted an eyelid if her daughter had turned up at her door at 10 o'clock at night, as long as she knew where she was and with whom she was, and at what time she was returning home. Today, however, she was seeing her daughter's arrival through a different set of lenses. In fact, through the lenses of Miriam's future in-laws, through the parents of the man with whom Miriam was engaged with. It didn't somehow look very good for their daughter to arrive home at such a time by herself and dressed as she was.

In one glance she took in her daughter's appearance. The clothes which her daughter regularly got in and out of — jeans, blouses, jump suits and which wouldn't have aroused her interest normally, today stood out brazenly on Miriam's body. She couldn't quite make herself understand why but she felt ashamed of her daughter's clothing and was angry with her, for compromising herself in such a situation. To think Miriam's in-laws had seen her dressed like that. She wanted to quickly usher her out of sight. With her eyes she signalled to her daughter to go upstairs and change into something more respectable. Miriam understood her message immediately. She was only too glad to oblige.

Squeezing past her mother and out of sight of their guests who had now entered their living room, Miriam almost ran up the stairs to her room. Once there, she closed the door behind her, and breathed out deeply. Her earlier feeling of tiredness and exhilaration from the hill walking had vanished and discontent had taken its place. That was another world. One that she had left behind as she waved good bye to her two friends on the bus. What mattered now were the two people downstairs. And they mattered! Her future lay with them.

Going further into the room she peeled off her jacket and the pair of jeans. Now cluttered on the floor she looked at them with distaste. Her mouth twisted into a cynical line. Damn it! Her mind shouted. 'They are only clothes. I am still the same person, the girl who they visited regularly —

the person whom they chose as a bride for their son in their household'.

Deny it as much as you like, Miriam, her heart whispered. It's no use. They have seen another aspect of you. One that had apparently, by sheer accident or sheer contrivance, remained hidden from them from the very beginning. When they first saw her at a party, she was dressed in a maroon chiffon sari and later on each occasion she was always smartly but discreetly and respectably dressed in shalwar kameze suit. Never at any time had they glimpsed a jean-clad Miriam. It must have been quite a revelation to them. In fact, judging by her mother's expression and lack of composure, a nasty shock! For now, they were seeing her as a young college woman who was very much under the western influence. One who dressed like English girls.

After all no decent muslim girls would go outdoors dressed like that, especially in the short jacket, which did not even cover her hips. She had heard of stories about in-laws who were prejudiced against such girls. Ones who feared and avoided having such daughter-in-laws, because they brought havoc to their households. For they weren't the docile, the obedient and sweet daughter-in-laws that they preferred. On the contrary, they were the rebellious upstarts who did not respect either their husbands or in-laws. Miriam knew about the stereotyped views of such women.

From her wardrobe she drew out a blue crepe shalwar kameze suit. As she put it on, she found the thought of them distasteful. They were only articles of clothing, but having them on her back she had embraced a new set of values, a new personality in fact. With a quick glance in the mirror she left her room. As she went down the stairs, she felt a new person. Instead of scuttling down the stairs, she was now fully in control of herself. The long scarf, 'Dupatta' was draped around her shoulders and one edge of it casually covered her head.

Once downstairs in the hallway, she hesitated. She felt sick at her hypocrisy. She was now acting out a role, the role that her future in-laws preferred. A role of a demure and elegant bride and daughter-in-law. Yet she was the same person who had earlier traipsed the Pennine countryside in a pair of jeans and wellingtons, and who was now dressed in the height of Indian fashion. The difference lay in what her in-laws regarded as an acceptable mode of dress. Or was she the same person? She didn't know. Perhaps those views were right, and there were two sides to her character. A person who spontaneously switched from one scene to another, from one mode of dress into another. Now, dressed as she was, she was part and parcel of another world; part of a muslim Asian environment. She was now on home ground, and her thoughts, actions and feelings had altered accordingly.

Once inside the living room, Miriam felt four pairs of eyes turn in her direction. She stared ahead knowing instinctively that apart from her father they were all comparing her present demure appearance with her earlier hoyden one. She moved around the room at ease, in a manner that she could never have done in a hundred years in a pair of jeans amongst these people. She sat down beside her mother, aware of her mother-in-law's eyes assessing her appearance and movements.

After a while, conversation between the two sets of parents flagged. Fatima was doing her best to revive a number of topics of interest to the other couple. The latter, however, seemed to shy away from the topics, particularly the one concerning their children's marriage in six months time. Miriam noticed that the guests were ill at ease. It was so unlike their usual behaviour. There were moments too, when husband and wife exchanged surreptitious glances. Fatima became worried. From the moment her guests had arrived she sensed intuitively that something was wrong. She was ready to broach the subject with them. But first she asked her daughter to bring in the refreshments.

Miriam left the room in hushed silence. She pottered around the kitchen, collecting bits and pieces of crockery from the cupboards. Her own earlier hunger was nowhere to be felt. The appearance of those two people had done a miraculous thing to her metabolic system. She just finished arranging the plates and glasses on the tray when she heard them leave the living room. They were saying good-bye to her parents in the hallway. Miriam was surprised. Were they going already? Why, they hadn't eaten anything. She called to them. The mother-in-law turned and smiled. They were in a hurry to get home, because they had guests there, she said. That was a lousy excuse, Miriam thought. If they had guests at home, why did they bother to come in the first place, anyway? Still dwelling on the subject she returned to the kitchen and put the tray on the table; what a waste of time!

The two parents-in-law walked to their car in silence. Once inside neither of them said anything. They both travelled in silence to their home, both lost in their own thoughts. They didn't need to communicate verbally. Somehow they could guess what each other was thinking about. On reaching home, the so- called guests to whom Begum referred to earlier had apparently gone. Their elder son, Farook was not yet in. The younger was apparently in studying for his 'O' level mocks. They could hear the radio blaring away as he listened to the pop songs at the same time as revising for the exam.

Ayub, having shed off his jacket and hung it in the hallway went straight to the living room. Begum followed him, removing her chadar at the same time. Ayub switched on the television and sat down in his armchair to watch. Begum stood in the room listlessly for a minute and looked at her husband. Then folding her chadar into its customary folds, she left the room and went upstairs to her bedroom to place it in her wardrobe. Having done that, she returned to the living room. She sat down on the sofa opposite her husband and waited for him to say something. The seconds ticked away into minutes, however, and he still made no move to say anything. She picked up the newspaper 'Daily Jang' from the coffee table, and began to read it, pretending to read it, in fact, to be more precise.

Ayub got up and switched off the television. Sitting down once more in his chair he looked pointedly at his wife, 'Well'.

Begum pretended not to hear him or understand the implication of his exclamation 'well'. Now that the moment of reckoning had arrived, she absurdly wanted to prevaricate.

'Well, what?' she responded, watching her husband over the edge of the newspaper.

'You know very well what I mean. Don't pretend to misunderstand me'. He rasped under his breath.

Begum examined the harsh outlines of her husband's unsmiling face. She did not know what to say, or how to say it, although she knew what he was referring to. She remained silent, staring at him.

'Well, what do you think of your future daughter-in-law? I thought you told me that she was very 'sharif', a very modest girl'.

'I am sure she is'. Begum persisted, feeling hedged, because she was the one who had chosen and took a liking to Miriam.

'Huh!' Ayub grunted. 'Sharif! dressed like that! Walking out like that late in the evening by herself. God knows who has seen her dressed like a hippy. Would you like any of your friends and relatives to see her as she appeared today?'

'But she's a college student — college students do dress like that. Haven't you yourself joked about tatty jean-clad university students?'

Begum wanted to excuse Miriam's mode of dress to herself and to him, although she knew she was not going to make a success of it because she agreed with her husband.

'Tell me, would you be proud to own her as your daughter-in-law? I know I am not. You talk about her being a college student. Well, do you know what sort of company that she might be keeping. You've only seen her at odd times, and always at home. Do you know what she is really like? Have you thought of the influence she could have in your household? Such girls want a lot of freedom. In fact, they want to lead their lives the way that their English college friends do. Did you notice what time she came in? Do you expect her to change overnight in order to suit us, people form habits. Are you prepared for a daughter-in-law who goes in and out of the house whenever she feels like it, and dresses like that? Can you guarantee that she will not have a strong influence on your son?'

He paused, waiting for her to say something. When she did not, he continued.

'You know of a number of cases where the educated, the so-called modern girls twine their husbands around their little fingers, and expect them to dance to their tunes. Are you prepared to lose your son to your daughter-in-law?'

Begum listened quietly to her husband's angry lecture. Deep down in her heart she agreed with much of what he said, but she was reluctant to show it. She hadn't anticipated the direction towards which the conversation was heading. And she didn't like it. After 25 years of marriage, she could read him like a book. She had already jumped ahead; with a sinking heart she guessed the conclusion, the outcome of this discussion.

She did not know what to think, or how to react. She didn't disagree with him over anything. Not one jot. She herself had reacted in the same way towards Miriam as Ayub had done, this evening. When she saw her standing near the garden gate similar thoughts had whizzed through her mind, although she would not have voiced them in such a way. Her womanly intuition as to what her daughter-in-law should be like did not quite tally with the picture that Miriam presented to them or to the picture that Ayub's words had conjured up. She'd never visualised her prospective daughter-in-law in a pair of jeans. She always reckoned on a conventional sort of a daughter-in-law. Definitely not one who was influenced by western form of dress, culture or feminist ideas as Miriam probably was.

What about Farook? How would they deal with him? Luckily, it was not Farook who had chosen Miriam, but she herself. A glimpse of Miriam at a Mehndi party (hen party), had tugged at Begum's heart. From the very start she saw her as the epitome of what her future daughter-in-law should be like. She was young, beautiful and well educated. She'd just obtained 3 'A' levels, at high grades, and in September was going to embark on some sort of course at the Polytechnic.

Begum had liked the way Miriam had acted — ever so correctly and gracefully. Above all she had liked the way Miriam dressed herself. After today's event, that was quite ironic. It was the way the black chiffon sari seemed to hug her figure gracefully, and her hair wound up so elegantly in a knot at the top of her head. She was not over-dressed or over-decked in jewels and make- up as some of her peers were wont to be. Nor for that matter was she over-boisterous and making a fool of herself. In short, she did everything that was correct and which appealed to her. Somehow she'd stood out apart from the other girls. Looking back now, two years later, Begum was sure that, not her son, but she herself had fallen in love with Miriam. She had even liked the name 'Miriam'. It was an unusual, biblical name, with a special ring to it. She loved using it.

From the very first, also, Begum had taken a liking to Miriam's parents, especially her mother. And liking one's in-laws, particularly the mother was an important matter. She knew of cases where the two mother-in-laws hated each other's guts and never quite got on with each other. Begum, and Miriam's mother Fatima met for the first time at that Mehndi party. After that they met frequently at each other's homes. With the subject of their growing children looming in their domestic horizons, the two mothers had naturally talked about the marriage prospects of their children.

Farook and Miriam met each other often, accompanied by their parents and they too, took a liking to each other. They found they were very compatible and suited one another. When their parents suggested to them, whether they would like to marry one another, both agreed heartily. Soon afterwards an engagement party was held for the two. In order to let them complete their respective courses, the wedding was to be postponed for a year or so.

That was a year ago. Today Farook's parents went to meet Miriam's parents in order to discuss the arrangements for the forthcoming wedding in two months time. They were to decide on the date and the venue and the arrangements to be made for the reception.

They returned home, however, without having brought up the subject of the wedding. Their thoughts were centred on the subject of their son's wedding, but more importantly on Miriam herself.

'Well', Ayub's prompting exclamation brought her to the present.

She turned to look at her husband once more and waited for him to finish what he was going to say.

'What are you going to do?'

This time she could not pretend to misunderstand him.

She faced him squarely. Yet as she was about to say the words her heart sank. She saw Miriam disappearing from her horizon. But then as she tried to clutch Miriam's image in her mind, there arose that one of her in that silly pair of faded jeans, and that ridiculous short jacket. It had to be. It was better to face the matter now than regret it later. The problem was how she, Begum, was going to solve the situation. She did not have the heart or the courage to play the part demanded of her, or the one that she inevitably had to play in this drama. Knowing her husband, she knew, he would leave it to her — to sort out the situation with the two parties; her son and Miriam and her family.

Once again she looked her husband directly in the eye.

'You truly don't want the wedding to go on then?' she tentatively asked.

'I thought I had already made myself obvious. What do you think?..'

'I suppose I agree with what you say, but how are we going to go about it?'

'I leave that to you — especially as you were the one hot on the girl. I am sure we can find lots of other girls for our son, just as her parents will find a man more suited to her standard than we are...'

They heard the front door open. That must be Farook. They stopped talking. Begum dreaded talking to him about Miriam. She got up and went into the kitchen to prepare his dinner (as she entered the kitchen the thought occurred to her that she would have liked Miriam in her kitchen). Ayub picked up the newspaper and began to read it.

Miriam had just got in from college, when she heard the 'phone ringing. She dashed down from her room to answer it. It was Aunt Begum, Miriam's speech faltered slightly when she found out who it was at the other end. She quickly obliged Begum in her request to speak to her mother. Miriam called her mother. Leaving the 'phone she went into the living room and sat down to watch television.

Fatima left the meal she was preparing and went to speak to Begum. They talked for nearly five minutes. There were moments of awkward silences and hesitations on either side of the telephone wire. By the time the conversation ended there was a pinched look around Fatima's mouth.

Begum said her goodbye in an uncomfortable tone. Fatima had quite literally forgotten to return the greeting at the end, but silently put the receiver down. Her eyes stared at the 'phone.

At the other end of the 'phone, Begum thanked god that it was over and done with. She sank down on the stairs. She felt bad, oh, god, she felt terrible. She had hated every minute of that conversation. Putting herself in Fatima's position, she realised how painful it must be for her. How would she feel if she were in Fatima's place, and found out that her daughter was to be bunked at the last minute?

Mechanically, as if in a daze, and with a hand to her temple, Fatima went into the living room. Going to the sofa, she sat and pushing the cushion aside absent-mindedly she stared in front of her, at the fireplace.

Miriam did not notice anything unusual about her mother until she realised that her mother had not said a word since she entered the room. 'What did Aunt Begum say?' she asked quietly.

'I - I', Fatima stammered as she sought an answer to her daughter's question. Seeing her for the first time since she entered the room Fatima was not yet ready to divulge what she learnt. She was still reeling from shock herself. Seeing her daughter she was further upset.

'What is it, mother?' Miriam's heart was beating rapidly, although she didn't know why it should. 'What did Aunt Begum say?' she asked again.

Unable to control herself any longer Fatima burst out with, **'She said that your engagement had to be broken off!'**

The area around Miriam's mouth paled. Her heart now in the pit of her stomach. 'Why, mother ?' she said quietly. She was amazed at how clearly her mind was functioning, although a buzzing sound seemed to hammer in her head.

'She said that they came yesterday to inform us, but found it impossible to get around to doing so. Begum says that her sister insists that her daughter marry Farook. It would be amongst the relatives then, and also they were well-matched together. She says she is very sorry and apologises, but her sister comes first'.

'What a lousy excuse!' Miriam's mind screamed, but she uttered not a word, and left the room.

She went upstairs to her bedroom, and closed the door behind her. Standing in the middle of the room, she drew in a deep breath.

Where was this sister? Why was it she was never heard of before.

'Not to marry Farook?' Miriam voiced loudly. Why, only yesterday she was planning how they were going to lead their lives together, after they got married.

Her mouth twisted into a cynical line. In her heart she knew. From the first moment she saw them that night, she had a dreadful premonition. She had known, although she had denied it emphatically to herself, that something was wrong.

The buzzing sound was still there in her head. Going to her wardrobe she opened it and looked inside. Her eyes sought wildly for something and her hands rummaged through the clothes and the hangers, until she found what she was seeking.

She drew out the repugnant looking article and threw it on the floor, as if it burned her to hold it. She stared at it, as if mesmerised by it. Then with her foot she gave it a vicious kick. Her mouth resumed its cynical twist. Her friends would never believe her if she told them.

The shabby looking and much worn pair of jeans lay nonchalantly near the end of the bed, blissfully unaware of the havoc it had created in the life of its wearer.

Third Time Lucky

Alice Sky

'Mum,' Paul began again, as Carla wielded her clumsy way, with the shopping bags and the trolley, through the three sets of swing doors separating her flat from the landing where the lift was, 'Do you know what Michael Murray said about my new shoes?' Intent on her manoevres, Carla forgot to answer, but Paul was not easily deterred. 'Do you, mum? He said they weren't new, they were second-hand. That's not right mum, is it? What Michael Murray said — is it?'

'What? - er — no, I don't think so,' Carla vaguely replied, not sure if she had heard him correctly. They had reached the lifts.

'Good. I told him so. Mum? I'm the best jumper in my class - better than John. Do you want to see me jump now, mum? Do you mum? Eh mum? I bet you think I can't jump from here to over there mum, don't you? Mum, do you think I can't?' Paul fixed her with a gaze of luminous intensity, waiting earnestly for her reply. He stood in a square of golden light projected from the window onto the opposing wall. The hot rays of the sun streamed through the fine transparent flesh of his ears, setting them alight.

'Yes,' said Carla, hoping it was the right answer, and wiping beads of sweat from her upper lip. Paul immediately bounded out of the square of light onto a dark tile on the floor.

'See mum! I can! I told you I could. Mum, did you like my picture, eh mum? The one I did at school? Do you think it's good mum, eh? Do you think it's the best?...' and so on.

Paul had never stopped talking since first grasping the technique. Carla often blamed her glazed, semi-conscious condition upon this, recognising the same look in the eyes of any adult who had spent any time in his company. If hs ran out of subject matter, he merely began again. Perhaps because of this, her second child, Melissa, sitting stolidly in her trolley, was growing up silent as the grave and twice as unyielding.

'*But do you like it mum?*' Paul continued in the insistent tones of one accustomed to being ignored, but determined to pound his message home. 'The picture I did at school? Do you —'

'*Yes Paul, of course,*' Carla replied at last, pressing the lift button again irritably, five or six times. Where the hell was this lift anyway? She could hear faint groanings and rumblings in the distance like those of some great, laboured animal. But they were fourteen floors up, and the strain might have proved too much for it, yet again.

'Charlie Graham said that I can't count! I can mum, can't I? Up to ten? Listen mum. One, two...'

Fourteen floors! Someone in the council had evidently felt that they would enjoy the view. Or maybe that one day she would throw her whole family over the balcony, thereby saving the council the job of transferring them. At any rate, they had been installed there, just weeks before the policy of placing families in high-rise flats had been altogether stopped. That was over five years ago now. They had been on the transfer list for five years.

'Nine, ten! See mum! I can can't I? That was right mum wasn't it? I got it right, didn't I? Charlie Graham said that I couldn't! He was wrong, mum, wasn't he, eh? Mum, wasn't he wrong?'

'Paul,' said Carla in sudden desperation, 'Do be quiet, just for a little while — I can't hear myself think ... Look, if you're quiet just till we get to the ground, I'll buy you a lolly at the shop...' Paul's wonderful green-gold eyes lit up with avarice. At one time she would have shunned such tactics. During her first pregnancy, for instance, she had been primly convinced of the do's and don'ts of childcare.

'Will you mum? Honest mum? A black one or a green one?'

'Whatever you like,'

'I want a red one.'

'Yes, well, just be quiet, please. Or no lolly.'

Paul subsided, then cavorted aimlessly around the trolley.

At last the lift arrived and Carla manoeuvred them all carefully inside, into the muddy pool of urine on the floor. Carla stood, trying not to breathe too deeply as the doors heaved to and the lift set off on its long downwards haul. Paul traced a pattern in the urine with the toe of his shoe.

'Don't do that,' Carla said automatically. She had once worked out that she said just five or six things in an average day, repeated many times. 'Don't do that,' 'Put that down,' 'Eat it all up,' 'Just be quiet for a minute,' and 'Time for bed,'. That was it, mainly. The extent of her daily repertoire. Carla knew that somewhere deep inside her there was a fully formed sentence striving to get out. But the days were gone when she had the time or space to work a concept through to completion. That part of her brain was sealed away, but hopefully not dying. It might yet emerge, butterfly-like, from its chrysalis. God if *only* she were not pregnant again! Carla thought with sudden fervour. How *could* this have happened to her? No one had believed her at first. 'Nonsense love,' Kevin had said, 'You've got the coil,' as if she had somehow missed this essential point, and 'Nonsense dear,' her doctor had explained in the careful tones of one anxious to clear up any possible misunderstanding on her part, 'You've had the coil for several months now, you know,'. But the passing weeks had found her gazing mournfully at home pregnancy testing kits in chemist shops at which her husband would not even glance. This was his own special tactic for dealing with anything which generated a vague sense of unease. He had long ago stopped looking at either of the children. Then one day there had been incontrovertible proof. Kevin had blanched, then rallied heroically.

'Never mind, love,' he had said, 'We'll manage somehow.'

The lift groaned to a halt and the doors parted, protesting noisily. Paul bounced out, obviously bursting to speak.

'I can have my lolly now mum, can't I mum, eh mum?'

'Uh hmm,' Carla assented. She let him go on, answering him in a series of ambiguous mumbles which might mean anything.

It was funny, when you thought about it, how people

enjoyed stating and restating the obvious, then saying it again. Reactions to her pregnancy had varied from dismay to consternation. Most people, however, had felt a need to spell out the bleak details of her situation in case, presumably, they had escaped her.

'But I thought Kevin was going to be made redundant. Isn't the factory closing down?'

'Yes, that's right.'

'But that means he'll be out of work.'

'Yes,'

'Well there won't be much money, you know,' or, alternatively,

'But you've already got two,' as if she were talking about growing another leg.

'One of each,' in explanation, then, to make the concept crystal clear, 'A boy *and* a girl.'

Strange what a comfort simple reiteration seemed to be to some people.

Outside the sun was a simmering bowl of golden liquid. The streets steamed in the heat. Carla steered her way cautiously through the shopping crowds. She had told her mother last of all for some reason, in a little tea shop in the precinct.

'But, dear, is that wise?' she had asked tentatively.

'Oh Christ, mother, not you too,' Carla had thought, shredding her napkin into smaller and smaller pieces.

'I mean,' her mother had persisted, 'You do have two already — and there's the flat — and Kevin's job — ' Carla was silent, so her mother continued, warming to her theme. 'I mean, the children are quite a handful, aren't they? So I don't see why —'

'BECAUSE THE BLOODY COIL DIDN'T WORK, MOTHER!' Carla had boomed suddenly, to her own surprise. An astonished hush had descended on the tea room. 'IT DIDN'T SODDING WELL WORK AND NOW I'M GODAMN WELL PREGNANT!' She had bellowed, elucidating, ending on a high-pitched screech.

Carla detested shopping, encumbered as she was with bags and kids, so she finished as soon as possible, turning on her painfully slow process back to the flat. Paul was silenced this time by the largest lolly she could find.

She would die for her kids, of course she would. She would lie down right now in front of that oncoming lorry, in fact, if she thought anyone else would take care of them. But a third! She was doomed, she could see that now, to give birth at regular two year eight month intervals until death. Grim visions of herself walrus-like and obliterated by stretchmarks swarmed into her mind.

Inside once more, Carla was dismayed to see a rough notice tacked carelessly to the lift door — 'Out of order'.

'No. Oh god, no.' She breathed. Fourteen flights — 196 stairs. There was nothing for it, however, but to begin bumping and thudding her cargo slowly up the steps. At the end of the second flight, Carla sat down suddenly, tears brimming unexpectedly.

'What's the matter, mum?' Paul said, then, putting an arm around her neck, 'Don't cry mum, it's alright. We can sit here for a bit. Daddy's coming soon, mum, don't cry. He'll help us up the stairs.'

And I'll know my song well

Di Williams

'And you're unattached?' the man on the phone had asked.

Yes, she reassured herself as she waited in the station. No kids, no partner — she was now able to leave everything and tour, or sing on the cruise in their advert.

'We don't want any trouble from husbands, that sort of thing.'

That troubled her, and she hadn't liked something in the man's voice. If she'd been a man, they'd never have put it like that. She fought against fears of white slavery — no, that was just the man in the agency. But she could be exploited, and nobody would know about it. She'd have to fight her own battles, then. No classic male-protector figure. A male singer would, of course, fend for himself. And vocalists were two-a-penny, these days, male and female — still ripped off by the music business.

The thought jogged her memory, and she glimpsed the young man's puckered face as he worked out his guitar chords that summer. The hills reminded her, too of those near Bury where she'd given him a roof, and listened patiently to his outpourings, dreams, anger and disappointments. Singers were two a penny. Not that he'd had any time for her own music — he sneered at her practising — nor for her mounting musical frustration.

A car drove up. The studio was off the beaten track and she'd no car. With relief, she noted that both the musicians sounded nothing like the man on the phone.

The talk was straightforward and pleasantly intelligent, as

they drove past sprays of brambles on the hedgerows. Had she a good vocal range? Was she a reader?

She was cheered that they seemed interested, when she said she could read music. How fast did they have to learn songs? About a week, one said, to get a grasp of a song, but they could busk, many of the audience wouldn't understand the English. Chart material, he said, nothing too difficult.

Her heart sank a little. She had hoped for something more exciting, or in one field of music she felt a bit more affinity with. Most of the top ten was mindless disco music. She bit her lip. But she wanted the audition, if only for the challenge of singing something straight out, and seeing how the musicians worked. She wanted to prove she could work, too, and set out to take this job — worth it for the money, and she needed that, and a possible way up to more suitable work, useful experience.

It was refreshing to be given a task which stretched her, and she warmed to it when the music book was opened on the stand in front of her. The place was furnished with comfortable square seats, quiet grey, and the sound of voices had a pleasant, slightly hushed resonance. They had not said very much, one seeming to be reassuring, saying there was no time pressure, she could go over something more if need be, while the higher-voiced pianist gave her information about the song's structure, the tempo and prepared to start playing. They did, she noted, expect her to understand easily, as they did, a language of terms she didn't use. She found she got the sense of things quickly, with a small and excited adjustment — nothing was too obscure.

She came in well the first time by counting the bars, and was pleased with herself when she'd learned the tune by the last verse. She could put more expression in it.

'You could busk — go on for a bit,' the man on her left nodded at the pianist, who carried on into another verse.

This was fun, and she let herself range over the tune, bending and ornamenting it as she felt it, trying out a smooth, then husky tone in her voice.

The pianist ended then turned to another page. She had more difficulty with this one, and knew it must be obvious, as she smiled to stop herself frowning when she'd missed a bit. They started again, just once through, then the deeper-voiced man asked if there was a song in the sheet music that she knew. There were some, that she half-knew rather than could sing without looking, and one of these was a 60's pop song.

She knew she sounded a bit like the American singer — she was mimicking her — but the pianist closed his book afterwards and went off to make some coffee.

The other turned and started rooting through a box of cassettes. They are both much younger than me, she thought. They've always had good equipment, like that tape deck with all its controls. Any tapes she had of the old days were so crackly.

'This is something we were working on last year.' The dark man was smiling.

Good, she thought, warming to the unusual chords, even though she felt the smooth keyboard playing and the drum machine sounded a bit plastic.

'From the archives,' he said. 'We have put that aside, now we've taken this on.'

What a pity, she thought, disappointment surely showing on her face. She'd had the embryo of a tune, forming in her head over the music. She didn't dare to sing it but it was her secret wish they'd let her improvise to that tape, till he'd said that.

'Don't you want to play like that? — It's an interesting sound.'

The man gave a short laugh and explained it wasn't feasible from the money angle. The pianist came in with the coffee, and he put the cassette player off.

The next conversation was over all too soon, and she realised she was drinking the coffee for consolation. What they needed was really someone a bit more extrovert, to front the band, and not mind what kind of song was asked for. And, the pianist implied, a bit of a mover, someone like the kids on Top of the Pops. They thanked her for coming all this way, and hoped she'd find other people to work with, but the pianist said they were expecting another singer soon, and drove her to the station.

Sitting in the carriage, looking out over the hills with her eyes filling with tears, she tried to brush it aside as just another experience. They had been kind, and not patronising, had treated her as another musician. But that was the sting. She needed to work with musicians like that, needed to be stretched creatively. She needed it even more than just having some kind of a living. She wanted to earn a living through music, good music.

That tape they were throwing out — what a waste — had a tune that was still with her, welling up inside, ringing through her head. She ached with frustration and longed for more tunes, different instruments, even ones she'd never learn to play herself, to make the complex music she had in her mind. She wept.

There was no way she could go straight back to her empty flat. Outside the station she wandered down the steep hill and into a pub. She hoped her tears didn't show.

The juke box was off, and surrounded by lads in leather jackets, some fringed or studded, old emblems glinting on denim yokes and pockets. They had long hair, too.

'You don't mind them — they're a good crowd. Wellies, that's Hells Angels.'

The young woman next to her nodded in the direction of the juke box.

She found she was smiling to herself, and hoped that her spiky-haired young companion at the bar didn't notice. Hell's Angels — that reminded her of Bury again, and that was years ago. Where were they now, friends of those days — were they still all out of work?

Out of the corner of her eye she saw a hand pick up the neck of a guitar, and a wave of nostalgia made her turn away.

'Half a bitter, please.' It was all she could afford after the train fare.

The landlady shouted something to one of the lads, who was disappearing up the stairs, first to leave the now disbanding group.

'Having a session upstairs,' she explained, nodding towards a handwritten and blurred poster on a panel of the wall.

The moment of being torn between common-sense and adventure was short, and she found herself upstairs, amid dusty lamps and boxes, her glass in her hand.

There was a mike. I used to sing in rooms like this, she told herself — but no, Hell's Angels, they were in a different world.

She didn't know how it happened. Somehow, in the middle of a twelve-bar break on the one guitar, she was on her feet, and by the time she got to the front the mike was in her hand. Blues, the old blues, welled up inside her from everything she'd ever heard played, and from her own chest. The words didn't matter.

There was applause, breaking through her last note, and she stood there with the mike. Yes, she went on alone, through an old favourite of hers, on to something more like a chanting. They were all watching, and the end was noisy with their notes echoing the last phrase, and 'Yeah!'.

She gave the mike back to the guitarist and sat down.

He started playing, which was fine. She wanted to sit and recover, but there were wide-eyed and enthusiastic faces all round her.

'You sing on your own! No backing — that's amazing…'

'Got any more songs like that?'

She motioned them to listen to the guy performing, which they did without hesitating. He, too was smiling at her.

By the end of the song she found she was daydreaming, on a wave of nostalgia for those balmy summer nights. She brought herself back. These were just a crowd of ex-hippies, out of touch with the present. Like her. Wake up.

There was a nudge of her shoulder from behind. It was the punk-hair woman from the bar. Punks were also part of another era, she reminded herself.

'The landlady said she wants to see you.'

So she went down, a bit dazed, and learned there was different music each night of the week, and more than one group of musicians looking for a singer. Back on her stool upstairs, with a free pint, she hugged herself, at the start of a good run in her luck, it must be. She felt back on home ground, the first time for years with that tingling of excitement, as she was called to the mike again.

Bereavement

Peri Stanley

Physically, Theresa's suffering was caused by her sensitivity to the cold. But there was also her idea that she was really, and in any true sense of the word, dead. The thought of her brother's accident clung to her skin like damp clothing, yet somehow could not penetrate to the heart of her and when her sister-in-law had phoned to give her the news, all Theresa had been able to think of was the small cough tickling the back of her throat. The light in her room stayed on, however, day and night — her one concession to bereavement — because it frightened her to think of waking into darkness and into silence, as in a tomb.

Clenched near the electric heater, she glanced at her watch. Ten-thirty. It would soon be time to catch a bus to the funeral. Ten cigarettes, rolled in advance, lay in a neat row on the table and next to them a pile of matches, one of which she dashed at the wall until its pink head exploded. Her shoulder-blades felt tight with the cold.

Peter's arrival startled her. He thrust flowers through the doorway.

'I've come to offer condolences on behalf of everyone at the Centre. We were all very sorry to hear about your brother.'

His tone was mechanical, as though he had been made to learn the words by heart. Theresa did not think that a word like condolences would be part of his normal vocabulary.

'Do come in,' she said and then saw Peter eyeing the book that lay open in the armchair. How long had she been teaching him to read now? He was quite a fast learner.

His leather jacket and jeans, holed at the knees, appeared incongruous in the context of her room, filled as it was with the landlady's furniture. But he smiled and they found things to talk about while Theresa made tea. She fluttered in search of milk and sugar, her large body swathed in its mourning garments, animated at last.

'It's funny because I hardly ever saw Eddie, not since we were small children. That was my brother's name, Eddie. He chose to go with my father after the divorce, you see. I stayed with mum.'

'When's the funeral?' he asked.

'Peter, I can't face it.'

The way he had smiled at her just now had given Theresa confidence. She did not wish to stand beside a grave with people she hardly knew, where her absence of grief would be visible to the world and provoke a quiet loathing.

'I don't want to go to the funeral today,' she said.

'Well, I'm not making you.'

'Could we go for a walk or something?'

'I could do with some fresh air,' said Peter.

It was nice to walk beside a good-looking young man and Theresa considered whether they looked like a couple, even though she was so plain in comparison. Could other people tell that she was older than him?

They found themselves in a narrow lane that smelt of burnt wood.

'I'm surprised that you're so cool about your brother's death,' said Peter. 'Women are usually more upset by that sort of thing. Softer than men, aren't they?'

'Who told you that?'

'I thought it was common knowledge.'

Theresa encouraged him to talk about his plans for the future, for when he was properly free. Phrases culled from the social workers at the Centre sounded hollow in the boy's mouth. He was to return to his family home in Liverpool. to seek employment as a car mechanic. At the moment he had the worry of his car maintenance exams.

'It's beginning to get me down,' he commented.

Rats' teeth of cold gnawed at Theresa's nose and ears and

at the tips of her toes and fingers. She looked up over the hedge. Her own future seemed to unravel itself and stretch out over the fields in their shroud of frost. Behind her too lay endless, yearning acres of icy ground. The grass looked ashen, as though all its green had been sucked out. She could not help but define her life in terms of what she had failed to do. At the age of twenty-five, Theresa had not married or had children or found a paid job. Her virginity was quite intact.

She gravitated naturally towards the heat of Peter's body. It occurred to her that she had never before walked alone with a man along country lanes. Not unless you counted those outings with Dad and Eddie as a child. When Peter sat at the desk in the classroom at the Centre, Theresa conjured up images of him making love with girls. Always other girls, shaplier and more beautiful than herself, because it seemed an audacity to imagine she might ever occupy his thoughts in this way. But looking at him now, she knew she wanted to be with him, to feel the warmth of his weight on top of her. That was why she had broken the rules of the Centre by coming out here alone with him today. She lit another cigarette.

'You smoke too much.'

'I need something to hide behind, I suppose.'

Theresa wanted to cling to the flesh under his arms and kiss his lips. He climbed a fence and she followed him up into the light.

'How much d'you get paid at the Centre?' he asked.

'Nothing. I'm a voluntary worker.'

'Christ! You wouldn't catch me working for nothing!'

'It gives me something to do.'

Theresa winced and thought that what she said never pleased him. She felt locked within herself, struggling to communicate what she was in a sentence here and there. Noone ever seemed to allow her more than a sentence at a time, but she wished very much that she might blend and sway with things.

They marched slowly alongside a frozen stream.

'It's too cold,' he said. 'I know somewhere warm we can go.'

Minutes later he was leading her into the oily warmth of his hut and clearing a space between parts of engines. He lay across a blanket on the ground and closed his eyes, while Theresa knelt next to him. His face was at its most beautiful like this, quite still, and undisturbed by thought or emotion, except that there was the slightest hint of insolence. His blondness seemed to glow like a halo in the dark hut. Like Eddie when he fell out of the tree that time and lay unconscious while they waited for an ambulance. Peter's face was white and still and very separate from everything around it: not even an eyelash fluttered. Was that how her brother looked now, resting in his coffin?

Theresa could feel the tepid current of air from Peter's mouth. She could hear his breathing and also her own and the sound of her heart which throbbed now like a sick headache. Her hand thawed and trembled in mid-air for a while before it slid across the tatoo on the boy's upper arm and came to rest near his throat. His eyes looked expressionless as he pulled her closer to kiss her and his tongue danced hot inside her mouth. Hot saliva mixed with tobacco taste sent warmth oozing around her body, but there was still a part of her mind that remained cold. What would their grappling bodies look like to an independent observer?

It was as though Peter had asked himself the same question. Suddenly they were apart again and she lay on her side on the blanket, her mourning dress creased and rucked around her knees. There felt a huge space between her arms where Peter should have been. Theresa looked up at him.

'I'm sorry, but I can't do it. It doesn't seem right,' he said. 'It can't be right with your brother dead and a funeral going on.'

'Then why bring me here?'

'I don't know. It was your idea to start with. I thought it would be alright but ... you're strange.'

There was silence and after a while Theresa walked towards the door. She tried to stop herself, but in the end she had to turn back towards him.

'Peter, you won't tell anyone about this, will you?'

'There's nothing to tell, is there?' he said.

The Confinement

Rhoda Lamb

Rose opened her eyes and looked at her sleeping sisters. They were not much younger than herself. Rose was eleven, Mary was ten, Elsie was nine. She felt the scrawny foot of her brother Tom, he was just seven, and was lying at the foot of the bed. How the four of them managed to get any sleep was a miracle, — but manage they had to. Rose gave Tom a jab with her foot saying, 'Keep yer feet to yerself.' She then poked her two sisters saying, 'Weken up, you two, it's half past eight.'

'Ek, wer' late today', said Mary.

Rose had two other brothers, Cyril who was five, and Jimmy who was six. They slept in a single bed in the corner, in the same room. They were already up. Rose could hear them arguing. 'Am first at sink' said Jimmy.

Ger' out' answered Cyril. They then started fighting. Then she heard her mother's voice, 'Tha'll be no fightin' in this 'ouse this mornin',' she said, ''Urry down you three, 'ave bin callin' thee an hour,' then she went on, 'a dunno' want school board knockin' on this door, dost 'ear me?' School board was a man who called on houses, whose parents didn't send their children to school regularly — there was quite a fear of him in the neighbourhood.

They came down two stairs at a time, mam was generally a patient woman, but at times she could lose her temper and slap them. After a swill in cold water at the brown stone sink, they had the usual breakfast of jam and bread, followed by tea which seemed to have been stewing an hour.

'Mam' said Mary.

'Yes luv, what do yer want?' asked her mother.

'Can I ... can I...' she looked at her brothers and sisters, then whispered, 'Can I...'

'Ek what's wrong wi' yer?' said her mother, 'a thought they wer' supposed to be learnin' yer English at school and you said 'Can I' three bloody times, what *do* yer' want?'

Mary knew she had better speak now, or she wouldn't be having that much longing for a chocolate biscuit at school break.

'A wanna biscuit at break' she managed to blurt out.

'Where's money suppose' to be comin' from?' asked mam.

Mary knew her mother kept pennies in a jar in the cupboard, but before she could say anything, mam said, 'That's spoken fer and no-one puts a finga' in that there jar.'

'Who spoke fer it mam?' asked Tom, showing off what he had been learning at school.

'Just a figure of speech', Rose said loudly. Tom blinked, opened his mouth to answer, then decided not to.

Mam was pregnant with her seventh, although she had had a miscarriage last year and one a few years ago. Things hadn't been easy for the Thomas family; for a start, the marriage wasn't anything like perfect. Also, she'd had one pregnancy after another. Her husband, Jack, was a drinker and if he'd no money for drink, he'd sit and brood. Also, he was on the dole, and would be, for a long time. 'Why couldn't he stop drinking and have a pint pot of tea instead?' thought mam.

'It drowns me sorrows' he'd say.

'Aye' she thought, 'it might drown his sorrows, but it doesn't do much for me and the kids. You could pull your guts out washing, scrubbing, and the like, and you got no appreciation off Jack. Never mind, it's me duty, it's me life, and it's me lot. What else can I do?'

The children had got off to school at last. Jack had gone to the dole, the house was quiet. A passing train sent a vibration through the small house, and a vase shook on the dresser. A knock sounded at the front door.

'That'll be Ginnie Grant,' thought mam, 'funny how you can recognise a person's knock.' It was Ginnie.

'Yer couldn'a,' she started, but was interupted by mam.

'No, a couldn'a lend thee a cuppa sugar.'

'It wern't sugar a wanted, it were bread' said Ginnie looking a bit uncomfortable.

'Dost know Ginnie?' said mam, ''av six childer of me own, and I 'av to feed yours too?' then mam saw the funny side, and laughed, 'O' reet tha can hav' t'bread, I canna see yer go clemmed.' She bent to open the dresser cupboard. 'A canna bend much' she said patting her stomach. She got the remains of a loaf, and handed it to Ginnie.

'You'll be well blessed, they say 'God' sends a loaf of bread with every babby born' said Ginnie.

'Aye' thought mam, 'and you seem to be taking it! How's your Harry goin' on?' asked mam.

'Ee's o'reet, but he's like your Jack — always drunk,' said Ginnie.

'Funny how they can spend all their money, and they're drinkin' all neet, then they come home and do nowt — but pee all neet, it don't make sense do it?' said mam.

'No' said Ginnie, 'Bloody daft in't it.'

'There's a Jumble Sale at Church Hall on Friday night,' said Ginnie changing the subject, 'if yer not there a'll look for babby clothes and owt for't children.'

'I, o'reet,' said mam, 'I might be there meself, a'll see how I am.' Then she said, 'Oh, a'v just remembered, if tha sees Nellie, yer know, her at number seven on t'other side at street, would tha give her a knock and ask her to mek me that frock fer our Mary, she has material and t'measurements?'

'I o'reet a'l give her t'message.'

'Ta luv,' said mam.

'Well, a'll be off now, a'll call to see how yer going on through t'week, a'v me errands to do, dost tha want owt from t'shop whilst am goin'?' said Ginnie.

'No, a'm o'reet fer stuff.' Said mam.

'Ta ra then, thanks for t'bread, a'll let thee have it back' and Ginnie departed at last, much to mam's relief. She didn't feel well, and she didn't feel like any gossiping these days, and anyway Ginnie was always on the borrow. Mam didn't mind now and again but not two and three times in a week.

Rose turned the corner from school, she sensed something had happened. Mrs Morgan was talking to Mrs Brown, they stopped as Rose approached, although Rose's keen ears had caught the words confinement and labour.

'A think thee mam could do wi' thee,' said Mrs Morgan, 'She's not so well, cock.'

Rose dashed inside, mam was sat in the rocking chair by the fire. She looked pale, almost scared.

'Ee, Rose, a'm glad to see yer earlier today, a don't feel well.' She got out of the rocking chair, and sat on a chair near the table, leaning on the table, almost sending a bottle of milk over. Rose caught it just in time. 'A canna rest' said mam.

'What shall a do?' asked Rose, 'where's me dad?'

'Usual place, but he's best left there, he wouldna' be any use here,' said her mother wearily, 'Mrs Hope's gone for t'Doctor, she told me t'knock on t'wall if a needed owt, a good job she heard me.'

'For a start, get that brown paper and newspaper a put under t'stairs, get a clean sheet — nowt patched, and change bed, put paper over t'top of t'bottom sheet, yer know? I canna have Doctor Bray seeing a dirty bed.'

Rose set about her jobs. When she'd finished, she filled the kettle and put it on the fire. 'Dost want a cuppa tay mam?' she said.

'Aye' said her mother, 'yer a brick Rose — yiv' no need to go t'school this afternoon.' Rose liked school, but she knew her place was here today.

Mam lay on the bed, it had been brought downstairs, she was in labour.

'How does it feel?' asked Rose.

'Not so nice' said her mother, not wanting to frighten Rose.

Rose sat on a chair in the corner of the room, and they waited for Doctor Bray and Mrs Hope.

'Ek,' thought Rose, 'if this is what it's like, am not havin' any kids.' She was sorry for her mother, she knew at the tender age of eleven, what a rotten life her mother had. She was there on the night of the miscarriage, she would never forget it. Mrs Hope had said at the time: 'If yer mother 'adn'a bin stood on that chair doin' them there winders, she'd o' bin o'reet.' Rose also knew her father could have been better, he didn't do right by her mother. Other fathers took their children for walks and things like that, hers was in the beer house at every opportunity. Of course she knew other children's fathers were the same, but she wished hers wasn't one of them.

Mrs Hope had arrived with the Doctor. Rose asked could she stay in the room.

'Aye, a suppose so,' said Mrs Hope, 'yer shouldna really cock, but it'll learn thee summat and that canna be bad.'

Mrs Hope was helping the Doctor although she was more of a hindrance. Rose knew her mother didn't like anyone looking, and Mrs Hope seemed to be doing a lot of unnecessary looking. Rose knew her mother would be embarrassed, whether she was having a baby or not — Rose knew her mother.

The children arrived from school for their dinner. 'Go round t'back!' Rose shouted. She had put the bolt on the front door — a wise move. She quickly took command by giving Jimmy a sound slap.

'What did'st clout me fer, I did nowt?' he yelled.

'Yer don't poke yer finger through bread as soon as yer walk in' said Rose. He kicked her on the ankle and ran into the back yard, slamming the door hard, it shook the house. Mrs Hope came running into the room.

'You lot can be quiet!' she bellowed, and ran back.

Rose heard a sound outside, she ran into the yard and caught Jimmy peeing in the grid, her mother never allowed the boys to do that, as she would say: 'It smells in the summer.'

Rose gave him a clip on the ear. He half turned in surprise, and the pee missed her by inches.

'What's lavatory fer?' demanded Rose. He retorted by sticking out his tongue. 'Don't pull yer tongue out at me, yer face is funny enough.'

Incident forgotten, she set about making them something to eat.

Mary said, 'Where's me mam?'

'A'll tell thee later on' said Rose.

They generally ate in the living room, but the kitchen would suffice today, there was a small kitchen table they could all stand around.

'What's fer me dinner, not drippin' butties again?' asked Cyril, poking his finger in a tin of condensed milk and licking it.

'Yer not allowed to do that' stated Rose.

'Aye, but a like it — it's lovely.'

'So do I, but I never do that — it's dirty' argued Rose, 'Me mam's ill,' she went on, 'and yer have to behave yerself today.'

'What's up with me mam?' asked Tom, before Rose had time to answer he went on, 'why's me mam's belly big — is it catching, will mine go like that? If it does, I canna win t'race in school games.'

'Shut up and get yer dinner, then yer wunno be late fer school' Rose said, smiling to herself at his remarks.

They finished their dinner, bread and dripping and half of apple each. That was all Rose could find in the kitchen cupboard. After they had left for school, Rose tidied the small kitchen, washed the cups which were cracked and had seen better days, and as an afterthought, washed the dirty towel that they had all used that morning. She threw it over the line in the yard, she could not find the pegs. She then brought in a bucket of coal from the yard which she carried into the living room. Doctor Bray took it from her with the words: 'I thought that would have been your father's job?'

Rose sat on the chair in the corner, well out of the way of the activity going on around her, she started to read a comic, whilst listening to the proceedings.

'It'll be over soon', Doctor Bray stated at last.

'I hope so', thought Rose, if this is what her mother had called: 'bein' not so well' then her mother must have made an understatement. She heard her mother crying out and moaning, then the words: 'It's a breach!' She wondered what that meant, then all was quiet.

Rose glanced at the bed, her mother was lay on her side, eyes closed, breathing quietly. Mrs Hope was looking, not saying a word. Rose never heard the baby cry, then she realized that she never would.

'Wrap the child in that sheet', the Doctor told Mrs Hope.

Mrs Hope did so, and then placed the child in a drawer, which was to have been used as a makeshift crib.

'I'm very sorry, it's unfortunate Mrs Thomas.' The Doctor continued whilst turning to leave, 'I've my rounds to do, but I'll be calling back later.' He quietly shut the door behind him.

Mrs Hope started to change the bed and tidied round the room. Rose made some tea, she put an extra teaspoon of sugar in her mother's cup; in her childish mind she thought it might ease the situation a little.

'Here mam',she said, handing her mother the tea in the best cup that she could find.

'Thanks luv,' said her mother, 'look Rose yer know what's happened don't yer?'

'Aye', said Rose, lost for words.

Her mother continued, 'A were lookin' forward to t'baby, a know a'v all you lot, but still another babby in t'house would'a bin nice, these things happen, and it canna be 'elped.' A tear trickled out of the corner of her eye, and down her cheek. She brushed it away with the back of her hand.

'Was it a boy or a girl, mam?'

'A boy, luv, a boy', sighed her mother.

Rose looked at the still form, but she did not want to look at the baby properly.

The door opened, her father staggered in, singing.

'Give me a pinta good ol' Chesters and a'll show thee what a man I am' to the tune of 'Take me back to dear Old Blighty'. He stopped short, 'What the bleedin' 'ell's goin' on 'ere?'

Then he noticed Mrs Hope, and his eyes finally rested on his wife in bed.

'What yer in bed fer it's not yer time yet, what's up?' he asked.

Mrs Hope could contain herself no longer. 'You ought'a be ashamed of yerself, yer ask what's up — and yer wife's just had a still-birth.' Then she shut up. She realized it was really none of her business, but she felt sorry for Nellie and the children.

Jack sobered up quickly, he knew he had to draw the line somewhere. 'Mek thee mam some gruel', he said, turning to Rose, then he shouted, much to Mrs Hope and mam's surprise, 'Mek it ALL milk!'

Next day, the burial arrangements were discussed, not that there was any money for funerals, and this one was unexpected. It would take place when mam was fit enough to leave her bed. Rose, her parents and Mrs Hope would be present. The baby would be laid to rest in an orange box, which wasn't a rare thing in these hard days, although parents were ashamed of such poverty.

The day of the funeral came. They were all assembled, waiting to troop down the road to the Parish Church. Mr Hope would carry the orange box, and after delivering it to the church, would make his way home. He didn't like funerals. A doddering old vicar who didn't seem to give a bugger, took the short service. The small pathetic box was then lowered into the small grave. No headstone or inscription would be on the grave. The baby had been christened at home, Rose had had the honour of choosing a name. 'Sam' she had said, then, 'mam do yer think we'll ever see him, yer know, when we die?'
'Ee, I dunno', said mother. Then she began to wonder herself.
Rose's father overheard the conversation, 'Yer talk a load a rubbish wench, when yer dead, yer done fer — and that's that.'
'I only asked', mumbled Rose, feeling inadequate. Perhaps her father was right, he sounded very convincing, and the vicar hadn't mentioned anything about meeting Sam again, surely he would have known.
Mam did not think Rose talked a load of rubbish, she thought it was an intelligent question. It had set her wondering, and had given her some kind of comfort. She realized what an intelligent girl Rose was, and what a callous man Jack was.
They walked slowly home. Jack walked behind them as though he didn't belong. It was his normal behaviour. He disappeared, calling as he went, 'Just goin' round t'corner, a'll be home fer me tay.'

They knew round t'corner was another name for 'The Queens Arms' pub.

Mrs Hope stayed for a cup of tea, and a piece of fruit cake bought with some of the pennies in mam's jar. Mam gave Mrs Hope the black coat, that she had borrowed and told Rose not to forget to give Mrs Brown the black gloves she had lent Rose.

Events of the day were discussed. 'Well it were a blessing,' said Mrs Hope, her mouth bulging with cake, 'it were for t'best yer know,' then added, 'yiv enough kids Nellie.'

Mam said nothing, she was lost in thought, Rose didn't think it was the right thing to say and she happened to be one of the kids mam had had enough of. Also she would have liked a baby brother to push in his pram on Sundays.

'A'll go then,' said Mrs Hope, 'it were a nice bit o' cake that, fairly full o' fruit, did'st tha mek it theeself?'

'I bought it from t'corner shop, yer know full well I canna bake or owt like that, a'm only good at tator 'ash, and stews, cakes is beyond me', said mam.

'Well, best be off, a'll see thee Friday, a'll maybe give thee a knock if tha wants owt doin'. Ta ra luv!'

'Ta ta', said mam.

Mam was still quite weak after her confinement. It hadn't been an easy birth. She hadn't stayed the full fourteen days in bed, she was up on the eighth day. Rose stayed at home to help, and mam lay on the sofa a few hours each day. She'd wanted the bed back where it belonged, upstairs.

'An't it bin awful day, mam?' said Rose, 'yer know, t'funeral and that, it depresses me.'

'Aye, it has that, and yer shouldna be depressed at your age,' said her mother, 'never mind, come on, cheer up, yer know I couldna got through t'birth without yer help, yer were a brick.'

'Couldn't yer mam? I din't do much, I couldn't, I din't know what to do', said Rose.

The children came in from school — no thoughts of funerals.

'I won, I won t'race at school. I did, and they gave me

a tanner, Mr Bowles give it to me?' exclaimed Tom.

'Come here, lad, let's give thee a kiss', said mam.

'I bought thee summat — a present.' And a grimy hand, held out a bar of chocolate.

'Well I don't know,' said mam, then a thought passed through her head, 'I bet little 'un they'd just buried would have just looked like Tom.' She quickly dismissed the thought, she'd six kids and they wanted their tea. Rose would help her. Jack still hadn't arrived home: of course when you've a second home...

Mam had gone to the trouble of getting a tin of best salmon, a jelly and a tin of pineapple chunks. Like Rose had said, it hadn't been a nice day, but they would have a nice tea, of course there was only twopence left in the jar.

After tea, Rose washed up with the help of Cyril; Mary and Elsie tidied up in the living room. Then they sat round the fire. Tom wanted to go out and spend the rest of his sixpence and to have a game of football. Mam wouldn't let him out to play, she said it wasn't respectful. Then she started telling the children of the old days when she was little and her mother was alive. Rose told her mother what Tom had said about 'Are big bellies catchin?'

Mam said, 'Aye they are — I catch 'em.'

The children started giggling. Tom didn't know what the joke was. Rose was hysterical, and mam laughed so much at Tom's puzzled face and Rose's high-pitched laughter, a tear trickled out of the corner of her eye and down her cheek — it was a tear of joy and she brushed it away with the back of her hand.

Nothing Happened

Liz Tolan

7.15 a.m. Standing at the bedroom window observing blackbird behaviour, I notice a neighbour dusting her dustbin. It's Mrs. Macey. And, significantly, there seem to be gargoyles at the corners of her roof. This must be a trick of the early morning light on some misshapen guttering. Below the gargoyles, frondy plants are tapping on Mrs. Macey's landing window. From the inside. Trying to get out.

I don't like being called Dorothy. It's an old-fashioned name. My parents were old-fashioned and kept me in white ankle socks until well into my teens. This may explain a lot about my subsequent development. Or, on the other hand, it may be entirely irrelevant. I don't like being called Dot either. I am currently unemployed.

8 a.m. Food. I'm experimenting with something brown and pelleted from a box whose front depicts a country scene. For the sake of my bowels. The pellets stick to the roof of my mouth, however much semi-skimmed milk I pour over them, before finally disintegrating. I like living alone — you don't have to worry about arranging food for others. My first husband would probably have flung the pellets out and flung abuse after them. Not realising they were only trying to do him good. He had many faults, but it was the briskness with which he stirred his cup of tea, as if trying to create a whirlpool, which I finally could not stand. Now for a nice green apple and a thick cup of coffee. Well, thick coffee but a fairly thin cup. Down the road at Sheena's house the cups are thick. She makes them herself at her Pottery Workshop. They are so thick you can hardly get your lips round them. I think life is difficult enough without this sort of obstacle to everyday events.

I find life difficult to digest. Sometimes I can't take it in at all. What if it all turned out to be an elaborate hoax? I go around with a wry half-smile on my face just to let them know I'm in on the joke.

10 a.m. It must be, at the very least. I'm wearing my smile, now, on the way to the letterbox to post some letters. I'm writing to my local Councillor and to my Member of Parliament. It's about the dog situation and it isn't funny.

I listened to Councillor Clough at a public meeting recently. He announced that the situation was polarizing backwards. I looked around. Everyone else was wearing a serious face. Some were even frowning. I had to go to the toilet for a good laugh. I couldn't stop the tears streaming down my face. I was still damp when I emerged. At the sight of Councillor Clough and his false — presumably — beard, I lost control again. I blamed it on allergic rhinitis, which impressed several people, and had to be taken home by Sheena, who was responsible for my being there in the first place. Sheena is very concerned, though not about me since she discovered I was only laughing. She was annoyed at missing the show of hands.

Anyway, I'm writing to Councillor Clough, formally, with copies, and to my Member, to ask them to do something about the dogs. I want them to stop shitting on my doorstep.

11.15 a.m. Clip clip clip. I'm cutting my hedge. Having posted my letters, I'm clipping my privet into an undulating shape with rounded sides. All the neighbouring ones are box-shaped. I could probably shape it into some sort of animal, a camel (or dromedary), hippopotamus, giraffe! It would take some time. Years. And possibly a wire infrastructure to encourage and support new growth.

'You'll get big muscles,' comments a passing man.

'Ha-ha, yes I will,' I reply.

Round about 1 p.m. More food. As I browse through the kitchen a lot of greenery finds its way onto my plate — lettuce, cucumber, watercress, sprouting seeds. I chomp through a mound of this undergrowth before deciding on a peanut butter sandwich for my lunch and a nice cup of tea. And a chocolate biscuit.

While lunching I am doing some more filling in of my form. It has taken several days already. I am applying for a job. I hope to become a cleaner at the local D.H.S.S. Office. I may have to sign the Official Secrets Act. The form asks for details of my parentage and Mother's maiden name. Also details of spouse or spouses if I am or ever have been married. I have been. Twice. The second one was a foreign national and not a British protected person or Commonwealth citizen. I fear this may go against me in the employment stakes. I may not be selected for interview simply because of this fact.

Despite the exotic gifts and pistachio nuts which he showered upon me I could not stand his overbearing and possessive manner. But when I packed his cashmere jumpers and fourteen pairs of white socks into his rucksack, he left without a word.

I can no longer understand the urge to wed which possessed me in my youth.

2.30 p.m. It is hot. Hot but breezy. I am exposing a lot of myself to the sun, on a checked blanket, on the front doorstep. Foolishly unprotected, I am laying myself open to the harmful rays. I can almost hear myself shrivel. But I want my legs to go brown. I have my sketch pad and some pencils in front of me so as not to seem idle.

I am an artist. I have a hat with a dead mouse on the brim to authenticate this claim, but it is on top of a wardrobe covered in fluff and cobwebs. I paint portraits of house plants and houses, but not of people, who won't keep still for so long. Occasionally, when I can afford some frames, my works go on sale along Sheena's pots at a nearby Crafty shop.

I haven't yet fulfilled my early promise.

3.30 p.m. My legs aren't brown but my face is red and I'm somewhat sticky and there are bits of several insects clinging to my anatomy. I've had to come in for a wash. And while I'm here I may as well have a little tidy up. Rearrange the piles of clothes in the bedroom and shake the duvet about.

Teatime. I don't feel very hungry. I've been looking out of the window at people passing by. I saw a suspicious character crossing the grass over the road so I memorized his appearance for future reference, but forgot to note the exact time. His hair was astonishingly red and his clothes were light in colour. And his jacket had side vents, Officer, yes, of that I am quite certain. The clinching piece of evidence — the oatmeal jacket with out of fashion side vents. I knew, of course, the minute I saw him, that he was the one. The one about to commit the awful crime.

8 p.m. I'm sitting in the kitchen with a library book with the door open for the evening sunlight. My fridge has been acting very loudly lately, working itself up into a frenzy then shuddering into silence — a sort of orgasm. I think it is because it is old and has to work harder to keep up the pace. I know how it feels. My library book is about a woman of thirty two and her older lover and the imperfections of their relationship. The man's son appears too, to spice things up.
There's a lot of wuffing going on, making it difficult to concentrate.

8.45 p.m. Click-clack Clickety-clack. Some ladies shoes walking purposefully down the street.
Flap-flunk. Something drops through the letterbox onto the mat. It is a note from Sheena written on the back of a duplicated letter about school meals. It says she will not be calling round tonight.

9.07 p.m. I'm in the bath, studying the cobwebs in the corner of the ceiling and listening to the continuing wuffing outside.

10.30 p.m. I'm asleep and dreaming ... Mrs. Macey is hoovering her lawn. The gargoyles look down malevolently. A picnic is laid on the grass, trays of thick mugs on my tartan blanket. It is a garden party in honour of Me. My paintings are hailed as masterpieces. The whole neighbourhood and Councillor Clough are assembled and drinking sparkling apple juice from Sheena's mugs. A stranger sidles round the corner of the house and makes a beeline for me on the blanket. His hair is astonishingly red and he wears a light coloured outfit. I am unable to move. . . .

Sometime. Blackbird song fills the air.

A Day in the Country

Alison Thorpe

I had often seen him in the bar that summer. I was on holiday from college. The customers were the usual sort — fat, middle-aged men with beer guts and red, sweaty faces; young lads in jumpers and slacks hanging around the pool table; a couple in the corner by the window, holding hands and gazing dumbly at one another. Once one of the beer guts, a bit younger than the others, got a bit merry and tried to pull me over the counter towards him. 'Come on love, just a little kiss.' And I had to shout for Mike, the landlord to quieten him down. But it wasn't a rough place. I felt sorry for most of them, there was little else to do in a small market town in the middle of nowhere.

Richard was different — quiet spoken and polite, intelligent. Not like the others. He had a friend who drank coke with lime in it and I remember the first time he ordered it I thought it was a joke but it wasn't. One day he came in with a single red rose for me — he'd probably pinched it from someone's garden. I didn't know what to say, no one had ever given me flowers. I tried to laugh it off, unsuccessfully. I stuck it in an empty beer glass and spent the rest of the evening pretending it wasn't there.

The Royal Wedding and everyone was pissed and silly. I was working all day. I finally sat down with a drink I shouldn't have had at about six o'clock. I lit a cigarette, enjoying a relaxing five minutes to myself, with no one bothering me, asking for drinks or a bag of crisps or trying to grab my bum. Richard sat beside me. I think we talked about politics and how pathetic the wedding was, but wasn't it a good excuse to get pissed etcetera. He had asked me out before, but I'd always refused thinking it was something you did with people you were in love with or fancied. But I'd run out of excuses and in the end I said yes, adding that it was only platonic. 'Of course,' he said and I felt stupid for saying it.

He picked me up from the bus shelter at the top of my road the next day. It was very sunny, one of those days where the clouds look like puffs of smoke pushed out into the sky by some invisible chimney, yet hardly moving. We drove to the coast in a white car and I remember feeling very stiff, my senses alert yet unfocused.

We walked along a beach and past the arcades and stalls full of young men playing space invaders and fruit machines and girls chewing gum and smoking cigarettes. Clacton seemed to attract the worst of every bunch — the ugly and spotty, the loud and crude, and lots of podgy red and white flesh squeezed into cheap summer clothing. But what made me any better than them? I felt like a snob, and I didn't know what I was doing there. Richard was okay. I suppose we chatted but I don't remember what about. We walked further along the coast and then drove to a restaurant. It was one of those with a driveway and the menu in a little glass box on the stone wall outside. It looked too expensive and I would have been happier with a pizza or something, but he insisted and I didn't want to offend him.

I remember sitting in a lounge on a deep sofa with flowers on it, drinking Pils very quickly while we waited for our meal. Everything seemed to be over-patterned and I watched a lobster swimming in a small, green tank. I could feel a stream of alcohol rushing round my body in whirls and waterfalls, but I couldn't stop drinking.

I don't know how, but I found myself kissing him in a alcove. It was as if I'd suddenly woken up and found my body doing something my mind was unconnected with. Was this before or after we ate? I tried hard not to see what the bill came to. He bought me a little pottery hedgehog which I eventually threw away.

We seemed to walk a lot after that, maybe arm in arm like lovers, along country lanes and back to the sea. The cool air was sobering me up fast and I didn't know what to say to him.

Mercifully we were back at the car, and driving home. I was more or less sober as we left Clacton and all those people behind. Perhaps music was playing, I din't really care.

'Would you like to see where I grew up?' he asked.

I nodded. 'Yes, okay.'

'It's a special place, I don't show it to everyone.'

He drove the car slowly down a narrow stony path into some woodland. It was really quite pretty with leaves and undergrowth glinting in the sunlight and small clumps of flowers everywhere. We crossed a shallow stream over stepping stones and came to a small patch of open ground and sat down on the grass.

I remember him pushing me down, not hard, and saying, 'It's alright, I won't hurt you.'

I lay there staring up as he bent over me, expectantly. I tried not to look at his face, and looked up at the sky instead. But the sun was in my eyes. A voice somewhere in the back of my head was saying 'It isn't happening, it isn't happening, it isn't happening.' How could I have been so stupid? Did I really believe he was going to show me some childhood haunt? Why had I agreed? We could have stayed in the car and gone home. It seems pathetic now, but I didn't want to offend him, after the meal and everything. I saw a hand coming towards me and I lay rigid I was squirming inside as his hand stroked my cheek and moved down over my breasts and tried to force its way down the front of my jeans.

'I don't want to' I said feebly.

We were alone. No one would hear me if I screamed, if I could scream.

'I'll be very gentle, you won't even feel me go inside you.'

He thought I was some innocent virgin. How could I even begin to explain? I said no, and no again, and again, but it was like I wasn't there.

But he didn't do anything more. He just got up and walked back to the car. We drove back in silence, and he dropped me at the bus stop.

He didn't come to the pub after that. I thought he would

somehow, but I never saw him. I remember coming home for Christmas and going out with a boyfriend. It was someone's party, I forget who, at a hotel by the river. I recognised his face amongst the crowd. He was laughing with some friends I'd never seen before. I stared at him for a few moments, then looked away.

Later in the evening he stood quite close to me. We were both aware of the others' presence but our eyes never met. I turned to the boy I was with and said, 'Let's go home.'

Maidenhood, Motherhood, Womanhood

Su Andi

One assumes that I did as other girls of my age in their fifth year at secondary school. The only difference between me and them was that they all had boyfriends and I did not. I understand totally why this was the case, and never once questioned it. It was because I was 'coloured', and the times were still difficult for mixed-race relationships. So I contented myself with forming friendships with the boys. Though I didn't entirely wrap myself in an Agony Aunt mantle, they often turned to me to discuss the problems they were having with their girlfriends, who of course were also my best friends. I occasionally lent them money to take these very same girls to the local picture house. I knew that my life would not always be like this, for outside school I did have boyfriends. I wasn't exactly in demand, but my company was, occasionally, sought.

I had been in the city centre only once before, to go to Beat City — later renamed Stax — on Fountain Street. Dazzled by its mirrored walls and revolving globular central lights, similar to the ones they had in the Twenties. I was like a fish out of water. Despite all my years at dance school, I was unable to move to the fast tempo. I had been unable to relax and left totally disillusioned. Now I was to venture out again accompanied by my best friend Pat.

Why we chose the Majestic I don't remember now, for there were so many more we could have opted for. Certain ones were out right from the start because they were famed for their heavy drug scene, a scene in which neither Pat nor

I were interested. There was the Twisted Wheel and Heaven and Hell. There was Rails on Cannon Street, though I learnt later that they did not admit 'coloured girls'. Jungfrau and the Roundtrees Group.

Pat's father was a racialist bigot so we couldn't meet at her house which would have suited both of us. In fact she could not admit that I was even a friend. Neither of us were permitted to be out later that 11pm, and I'm not sure that either of us wanted to stay out any later. We just wanted to sip at the 'Fountain of Life', which we were convinced flowed down the walls of some of these clubs.

Dare I really use the term 'those were the days'? Honey, you have never really 'Boogied-on-down', unless you lived during this time. The mid-sixties were the beginning of many things within the social sphere of life, both good and bad.

The newspapers, especially the Sundays like the News of the World were full of articles on drug taking.

'Black Bombers during All-Nighters'.

And the clubs did stay open all night. You could get a pass-out, which was a rubber stamp on your hand, which with skill and speed could be shared with another. This permitted you to leave the club for a time and re-enter without having to pay again. At 6am you were given a bowl of cornflakes for breakfast, I don't recall ever getting something to drink.

Young ears had already accepted the sounds of Ska and Soul with records like 'Al Capone', but it was not until the popularity of early Motown began to spread that Black Music became an acceptable form of listening. It was easy for the record companies to introduce the faster, heavier black rhythm into their recording, and for many American Artists it meant a popularity revival on the other side of the world.

It was on our third trip down to the Majestic that we met Stuart and Pete. Though Pat and Pete never hit it off, Stuart and I were immediately attracted to each other. Of a similar stature to myself we were perfectly matched and what was more important this guy had 'Soul'. He could move and groove in a style that even I could follow. At last I had found both a dance master and partner.

At the end of the night, well the end as far as Pat and I were concerned, we were each escorted to our respective bus stops. I hate to admit it but it took little persuasion on his part to get me to return to the club.

How innocent I was for a knowall. When the Police strolled through the place I was shocked, but not unnerved, for I had nothing to hide, apart from my age. So when I went rooting in my bag for a cigarette and pulled out a bottle of pills I was totally unprepared. I was all for handing them over to the Police when Stuart yanked me back to tell me they belonged to him. I sat rigid. My very first Townie and he was a Pillhead. As soon as the Police left I got up to go. Politely and sternly I thanked him for his company and told him to get lost. A few days later he turned up at school with a bunch of flowers. What twist of fate had made me admit to my real age for the first time I'll never know. Like any female I proved to be a sucker for romance. Stuart became my first love and our affair was to rush and pulsate with all the torrid passion that only first love can.

Mum took to him at once, well he was after all a decorator and she welcomed anyone who could do some work on the house. Likewise his family gave me a warm and genuine welcome.

Himself, Father, loved being cantankerous and not talking to anyone for days. It didn't take me long to work him out and to warm him to me. His greatest delight was to take Stuart and I down to the local to tutor us in the true art of drinking Guinness in a 'Sleeve' followed by a whisky chaser. Of course, the Guinness didn't taste as good as it did 'Back Home'.

Surrounded by all this warmth and affection, Stuart and I began to find it increasingly difficult to spend time alone together. Two young bodies quivering with desire and eager to spend our lust. We decided to go away on a dirty weekend to Southport. With Pete's help we booked a room, told our lies and set off.

Hotel is a bit of an exaggeration, for we wouldn't have dared to set foot inside a proper establishment. It was really a boarding house, run unfortunately for our needs by a 'mother figure'. She took one look at the pair of us and sent us upstairs to our unbooked separate rooms. We didn't have the courage to demand the double room we'd booked, so we slept apart. We spent the next day losing all our money in the amusement arcades, packed our bags and made an early departure.

Our return train was an express so we found ourselves in Manchester much earlier than expected. Over the loudspeaker we heard the announcement that the very same train would begin its return journey from that platform. We decided to travel to and fro so we could enjoy the privacy of the compartment.

Part of the train did go back to Southport, but not the section we had chosen to travel on. Our segment changed tracks and we found ourselves in Liverpool Lime Street. Besieged by panic we simply handed in our ticket butts and left the station. We had no money to speak of, and no idea of how we were going to get back home. We wandered the city like two lost children. As the darkness descended so our fears increased. Eventually more by error than determination, we found ourselves back at the station. The scene had changed dramatically, instead of the normal hustle and bustle of a city station, with its porters and ticket collectors controlling the crowds of passengers, now Police dogs and their handlers were performing the duty.

Stu acted quickly; seeing a party of men about to pass through the barrier to board, he bought me a platform ticket and told me to hide in a toilet. The train had already started to gather up speed before I heard him call out my name, and on reaching Victoria we merely left by transpassing a loading gate.

As the desire to spend all our time together increased I began to wag school. This resulted in a letter from my Headmaster asking for my removal. He had never been happy to accept me as a pupil in the first place. On my initial day he had requested my presence in his office to inform me that I was the first 'coloured pupil' in the school and to make sure I wasn't the last.

My mother pleaded with him, without disclosing her increasing concern about my behaviour and attitude. She spoke only of my continuous progress at school. Such diligence can only come from a mother. A mother who had spent the last twenty-four hours in blind terror.

With the knowledge that we had been found out, Stuart and I had decided to run away from home. Packing a suitcase and filling a flask of coffee, we had taken off into the night. We had absolutely no money till I managed to borrow some from the local Head Teddy Boy.

By the time I had fixed up the loan and we had speeded up to Central Station all but the local services had finished. We wandered around for hours till we came upon a building site. I think now it was probably a section of the Mancunian Way. We climbed inside a huge drainpipe — drainage pipe — covered the entrance to keep out the cruel night air and settled down. He slept at once but I couldn't, I kept on thinking about my mum and my lovely bed warmed by the electric blanket.

It seemed forever before dawn broke and I could see a filter of daybreak through the cracks of our barricade. We had to vacate our hideaway as quickly as possible before the workmen discovered us and possibly reported us to the Police.

We had a plan: Stuart would return to his job site to hand in his notice, collect his tools and most importantly any money owing to him. I waited in the park. I can still remember how cold and hungry I was. Worrying if my lips were as cracked and scum covered as his when he'd kissed me. Eventually he returned and we embarked on our first priority: feeding our stomachs. We had barely taken two steps when Mum and Auntie Jessie turned the corner.

I ran into her arms tears cascading down my cheeks. Once again I had proof of how much she loved me. Auntie Jessie gave us each one of her Kensitas and a short lecture. Then she turned to Mum.

'Come on, Peg, let's get these kids some breakfast, before they fall over. Then home for a bath and a sleep. They stink.'

Now, after all that, because of me, Mum was having to plead with a bigot who didn't have a true inkling of what kind of brat I was. With the help of the Truancy Officer, who seemed baffled by the harshness towards a first offender, she managed to get some leniency. I was to be given a reprieve for the period of one term following my return from the school trip to Norway.

Similar to my travelling companions I found Norway quite a boring place. I was unimpressed by the repeated views of Fjords that we were given on each and every trip. We were in a mountain chalet hotel which meant every evening was spent in the social hut adjacent, pumping money into the juke box.

One evening one of the girls announced that she was getting engaged when we got back. I told her in my best patronising maternal tone that I thought engagements at our age ridiculous. Why, we were only just turning sixteen. How did we really know that this was the person we wanted to spend the rest of our life with? What did we know about the world outside our little private sphere? We were mere children in a world of adults. I believed every word I spoke. For I spoke with a sincerity that was self-convincing. But I completely forgot every syllable when Stuart showed me my coming home gift and I slipped the three stone ring onto my wedding finger.

The announcement of our engagement was received with a fifty-fifty response, for and against. His parents were rather pleased. In early adolescence Stuart had fallen foul of the law resulting in a few stays at Her Majesty's College (Remand Homes etc). He was the only rebel in the family and therefore they were naturally anxious for him to settle down with the right sort of girl. I seemed to fit the bill. Especially as I was still determined to become a teacher. A profession that few parents could disapprove of.

Father's attitude? Well that's a story in itself! But please find it in your heart for a little sympathy for a man who marries not out of love but out of a sense of honour. Which is exactly what my father did. When Mother fell pregnant to one of his country men, who went to great lengths at court to disclaim his involvement, up came my father to tie the knot of marriage to a previous relationship that had barely glowed let alone blossomed. The stigma of unmarried motherhood was ten thousand times worse when the child was born 'half-caste'. Marry in haste and repent in leisure. How true in their case. At least the marriage had given him one thing, me. 'His heir apparent.'

To his neighbours and fellow workers here stood a man

who had taken on much more than the external clothing of his new country. He had become 'just like one of us', a hard working chap. And so he had for the latter. But deep in his heart my father had not forgotten one doctrine of his African upbringing.

Though he had entered into an inter-racial marriage and despite the fact it was now dissolved, there remained with him the commitment to do right by his children as the recognised Head of the Family. Had he been graced with a son he would have been duty bound to attend to his education and to guide him towards a marriage which would benefit both he and the family as a whole. Judge not this as primitive and unrealistic in these modern climes. In Africa there is no such thing as the extended family. We are all one family and we live our lives and work with the awareness of our family ties and commitments. To raise and guide the young, to care and ease the life of the elders.

In the case of a daughter, he has to ensure that she enters into a marriage to a man worthy of the title of Father to her children. A man of such standing that respect for him would be as natural an instinct as her willingness to serve and obey him.

From being a small child he had tried to drill into me one thought of heart and mind: that my marital future lay with an African. One particular time he tried to make his dream a reality. A fellow countryman told him a young man was in town suitable enough to be introduced to me. Sylvestor could only be described as the perfect scholar. He spoke seven languages and was at that time a student in Moscow. True when he spoke about his life in Russia I was fascinated, but whenever he attempted to talk on a more personal level I was petrified. He came for dinner about four times and each time my contribution to the conversation dwindled.

Whilst Dad cleared away the table he would invite me to the pictures. I longed to scream to him that this was not Africa. Marriages were not arranged between unwilling maidens and 'dirty old men'. 'This my good man, was England'. But how could I? I was too bloody scared then to do more than lower my head and mumble my refusal.

Dad was perturbed to say the least, and determined to

discover the truth behind my reluctance, as to why I would not play the hostess to this fitting young man. So he began to spy on me: thus he learnt about Stuart: and made plans to discover more.

By learning who Stuart's employers were he arranged to have some work done on his house. Stu recognised the address at once, but what could he do — absolutely nothing. Dad behaved perfectly normally, making him cups of tea, asking him how the work was progressing, how long it would take. Very subtly he turned the conversation round to a more personal level and began to enquire about his family and thoughts on life. So really, I should have been prepared when Dad in turn told me, that if I ever married Stuart there was every possibility that I would give birth to a disabled child.

It was a cruel, heart-breaking remark that had absolutely no foundation to it what so ever.

The tears flowed: how could he be so cold hearted? I told him there and then that one thing was for sure: I would rather never marry than marry an African like Sylvestor or even worse, him.

Mum knew better than to protest, that could possibly lead to rebellion and foolish behaviour. She was fond of Stuart, but she knew how his temper could rage with jealousy. Her one and only fear was that I might enter into a marriage as disastrous as her own. She had always strived towards success for her children, no matter what the price. With Campbell she had paid a long hard debt which even then was not settled.

Campbell had been born out of wedlock, within the walls of the only real home that my mother had known up till then. Knoll Park Orphanage, Liverpool. With my life I would swear that not once during those first four years of his life did she ever consider adoption for her son, born with no nose to speak of and a head bald 'cept for one long strand of hair down the back. She married my father to give her son a name. He received absolutely nothing more. My father did not have a liking, never mind a love, for the illegitimate brat of a 'lunatic'. Campbell's father had entered Prestwich hospital where he later died by his own hand.

I give you here no justification for my statement that Campbell was born before his time. In his 'inability to accept' the limitations that life set for him as a 'half-caste' child, Campbell was easy prey for the drug trade. Introduction came in his early teens and like a lost child it was destined to lead him by the hand on through the same doors of Prestwich Hospital numerous times.

There are many forms of institutions. Prison is one of them. Prison has become the inevitable temporary retreat of the drug user.

Years of imprisonment had given Campbell the opportunity and time to broaden his knowledge by expanding his scope of reading. Trouble was, he didn't really comprehend and thoroughly understand the depths of the books which he selected. Thus his head held a confused jumble of unrelated facts, which he would rearrange to fit in with his own doctrines and beliefs. With the coming of Michael X. and Malcolm X., the public indignation of the treatment of Angela Davis and the Soledad Brothers, Campbell became an Ego, unto himself. He would insist on quoting extracts from his readings. Who knows whether correctly or not?

'X's are the Dream Makers and we are the Weavers of Dreams.' That, I think, was meant to represent Michael X., Malcolm X., Campbell and others like him as one man.

With this 'gift' of knowledge and the fact that he himself was a conman, he was able to see through to the real Stuart. A visage which was not to become public for a few more years. Like Mum he was fond of him but he knew that I would be wasting my life if I stayed with him. And life, so he told me was too precious to waste. And who should know better than he having wasted so many years.

I *really loved* Stuart and spent most of my time telling him so. Now of course I wonder which one of us I was trying to convince. Wearing his ring was no assurance, because he knew that I didn't feel tied by it, I was prepared to walk wherever life led me.

'If you really loved me you'll prove it', he said.

'Okay,' I replied, as eager as he to be rid of my virginal trappings.

After our disastrous trip to Southport, we tried to ensure

that this time our plans were intact. He had a brother in Liverpool, who he felt sure would let us stay. Mum didn't object as we told her we also wanted to visit Knoll Park.

It was arranged that we would leave midday Friday and return on the last train on Sunday. We couldn't stop giggling. This was it. We were finally going to do IT.

I kept asking Stuart why he was so certain that his brother would let us sleep together. Because he never gave me a direct reply I kept on pestering him. Finally he confided that although he didn't really like Niggers, he never objected to someone screwing one!

I couldn't believe my ears. It wasn't what he was telling me, but the fact that he was telling me at all, even though I had forced him to tell. How could he ever hope for us to spend the rest of our lives together, when we had to face those sort of attitudes and prejudices from within our own families? It was no good. I could see no point in us carrying on. We were finished.

It was as easy as that. Too easy, maybe. Stuart held out his hand and I gave him back the ring. Silently he opened the front door and passed through it on to the garden and out of the gate. He paused for a second and I waited for him to look back. His body tilted slightly as he dropped the ring down the sewage drain, that's when I began to cry. I didn't want to finish with him, but I really thought I was doing the best thing for both of us. When true love comes, love that is going to last a lifetime, there should be no obstacles in the way. I was only sixteen remember: how was I to know that the course of true love never runs smoothly?

Life had taught me how to conceal my emotions and to get on with the day's task in hand. How many times had I arrived late for school after witnessing Campbell being sentenced yet once again. Yet, to all my school chums I'd appear no more harassed than someone who had overslept. I was convinced that he would recover and find someone else, someone more acceptable to all his family.

I was totally unprepared when a knock fell on the door a few hours later. When I opened it there was no one there, just a small package on the doorstep. I think now that I knew what it was before I reached out for it. I slipped the ring on my finger and shouted for him to come inside.

We decided to forgo our trip to Liverpool and rent a place in Manchester for the weekend. We scoured the papers till we found a flatlet at a price we could afford. Stuart made a quick and successful phone call and we were on our way. And my virginity was on its way out.

Our destination lay directly off Upper Chorlton Road. The taxi deposited us outside a block of what then would have been described as luxurious flats. We entered via a glass door ornated with wrought-iron work. It was so difficult to look old and mature for the grin on our faces. The man told us that it would only take him a minute to get the flat key and take us round. Greatly disappointed that this would not be our Nest of Love, I felt sure that it could only reflect that type of property which he rented.

We climbed silently into his car. It didn't seem to bother him that neither of us had spoken one word since our initial self introduction. Innocent fools that we were. Now that we had handed over the money — Oh, yes, we had already paid him — he wasn't in the least bit bothered whether we spoke again for the rest of our lives.

It didn't take long for the adrenalin to stop pumping as I noted the direction. We turned into Withington Road, stopping outside one of the huge houses that still stand there today. I knew this type of house of old. How often had I been embarrassed at Junior and Primary school when I went to see a friend. To discover that they were living — were they living? — in one room in houses similar to this on Monton Street.

He led us up and up the staircase till we reached a small landing on the loft. There was one narrow room with a skylight. Off this there was, well, you couldn't really call it a room, more a cubby hole. This contained a completely fitted kitchen consisting of a shallow cold water sink and a gas ring. The bathroom and toilet, he informed us, was communal two floors down. A cot bed, table and two chairs completed the fine furniture and fitments. Not bad for the grand sum of £5 per week! He hoped that Stuart would be comfortable and I prayed that we would, then he left.

We surveyed the two rooms like captives. Stuart suggested that he go out and buy some groceries. I said that we would go together for fish and chips and some canned drinks. I had no intention of being left alone there, never mind doing any cooking in our one battered milkpan.

It would never find a place in the journal of romantic locations, though we did spend most of the weekend in bed. This wasn't because I found sex to be the greatest discovery of my life. FAR FROM IT — after the initial discomfort of our first attempt at intercourse, I thought it a rather messy affair. Though anxious to learn more, dare I say even experiment a little, I remained unimpressed by all the controversy that had surrounded it. I did seek self improvement. Sometimes I would keep silent so that I could concentrate on everything. Other times I grunted and groaned, though I'm not at all sure if my timing was right, and still I was disappointed. No. We spent our time in bed because it was too cold to be anywhere else.

Trips to the toilet were chaperoned by either partner and then only out of necessity of nature. For the mere act of passing water we cautiously used the sink. You had to be careful for with it being so shallow it was apt to splash and you could soak yourself with your own wetting. Sunday morning couldn't arrrive too soon, once again an elicit weekend had ended in disaster.

Unfortunately when I discovered I was pregnant I didn't have a specially close friend-girl. I say unfortunately; for she might have advised me to seek the help and guidance of my mother, which would have saved me from the weeks of torment I had yet to face.

I didn't really believe that I was pregnant, still I loved all the intrigue that went with it. The suspected pregnancy!!! I was to learn that it was a very expensive game to play in every sense of the word.

The first outlay went on booze. You must know the Old Wives' tale. You sit in a hot bath and sip brandy, or is it gin, or whisky? Well we tried all three during those first weeks.

The second went on some large, black rubbery things with an obnoxious name. Not being too sure whether they were tablets or suppositories, I swallowed half and inserted the rest, and where they went is anyone's guess!

I knew quite a few girls locally and older girls from school who had, 'had to get' married. I also knew that only a small proportion had ended up successful, one or two had even finished with early separation and divorce. I was determined that this was not going to happen to Stuart and I. Giving him no reason at all I finished with him.

Maybe it was because I had taken him by complete surprise, or was I a better actress than I thought, performing with a cold heart. Whatever it was he didn't argue with me. (A long time after I learnt that he had attempted to committ suicide).

Now that I had dismissed Stuart from any responsibility he would have felt for me, I was able to give my full concentration to the task at hand.

I was beginning to gain weight rapidly. I was working at the local chippy and was getting to the stage when I could no longer fasten my overall. Mum never mentioned the increasing bulge, I hoped that she was living too close to me to notice, for others were already passing remarks. My next attempt at self-induced abortion, nearly proved to be our most dangerous.

I suddenly remembered dear, old, Slippery Elm Bark. Discovering it stinking in Mum's shop one day I had asked her what it was used for. She told me that people chewed it to try and draw stomach ulcers. Then she laughed and said that some stupid women inserted it in the hope that as it swelled the pointed end would pierce the womb, causing a miscarriage.

Then I got hold of some quinine. A source which I could no longer recall had told me that it had on one hundred plus percent success rate. That was it, how could I fail if I used the two?

In my darkened bedroom I went through all sorts of contortions trying to get that bloody piece of wood inside me. Definitely no longer a virgin, I still didn't really know where I was supposed to shove the thing. I would think that it had reached home, then as soon as I tried to walk about the sod would fall out. I cut some pieces thin, some thick. I tried long pieces with the hope of cutting off what excess protruded, and then I tried short little stumps. In the end I'd chopped up the whole lot with no success.

My only alternative was to fall back on the quinine by doubling the suggested dose. (I had already pledged to double the dosage as it was). I don't think it was pure quinine but from the way that it tasted it was 200% proof. You could swallow the stuff with no trouble, but then you were overcome with this amazing desire to burp, the biggest, the deepest burp of your life. Trouble was, do it one time too often and the whole lot would come back up again, bringing with it the entire contents of your stomach. Over the next few nights the results were fifty-fifty as to whether or not I managed to keep it down. But even if I had had a 100% success rate it would not have made the slightest difference. I was pregnant and pregnant I was going to stay.

The fact was, I was beginning to warm to the idea of motherhood, and once that thought had lodged in my head I could not move it. What had happened to bring this all about was an incident with a cushion. I had been sat reading a book in revision for my exams with a cushion resting between it and my stomach. Lifting the book for a closer look, suddenly the baby had kicked out and the cushion went flying through the air. Mum looked me straight in the eye. I didn't speak. Just picked up the cushion and sat down again. I HAD LIFE INSIDE ME.

She told me later that it had merely confirmed her worst suspicions.

The very next morning I received a letter from Stuart saying that he had met someone new and was moving down South with her. I broke down crying, the letter clasped in my hand. I had given him his freedom and I had sincerely wanted him to take it. Yet even with the life time memory I was soon to have of him I couldn't help shedding tears for the loss of my First Love. Mum walked up behind me and wrapped one arm round me, with her free hand she read the letter.

'And what do you want to do about your baby?'

'I want to keep it.'

'Well,' she said, 'we'd best start making plans. As long as you are sure you want to keep your baby I'd better get some knitting done fast.'

She could have screamed and shouted, a natural thing for

any mother to do. She could have told me to pack my things and get out, as many parents have and continue to do. To go, for she had troubles enough in her life. But she didn't. That was my MUM.

School had finally come to the final end-of-year term. It had been a hectic year, particularly the last two terms. Sitting exams for a start. Then the filling in for an absent gym mistress which meant organising and taking part in all the Saturday matches. I didn't really know how far I was, but what I did know for sure was that the crippling pains in my stomach at the end of each game, where not in my imagination.

It was now the end of July turning into August. For me they have remained two of the worst months in the year.

As a family it had been a close summer. Campbell was home from Strangeways and a feeling of peace seemed to prevail in the house, despite all the undercurrent of emotion.

It was Thursday. Auntie Jessie and the girls were coming over to visit. And as an escape I had arranged to babysit for the family across the road. I had been feeling very queasy all day and had told Mum I'd sooner, under the circumstances, keep company with a TV.

Four o'clock found me in bed with my stomach getting rapidly worse. Mum had told me to lie still, but I was scared and kept calling out to Campbell to go and fetch her. Suddenly the first labour pains hit me, bringing a scream of agony along with them. Campbell threw open the bedroom door in a fury. He had always had a fear of illness. Find yourself in bed with a slight chill and any chats you had with him were held with him stood with his head popped round the door, keeping his body free from contamination.

'Jesus. The way you're carrying on anyone would think you're having a baby.' As the pain subsided I could only offer a smirk in reply.

I'm not all that sure how much time passed. Mum and Auntie Jessie had gone across the road to substitute for me, which meant that there were less witnesses to the event. But Mum wanted to be absolutely sure that this was it before calling the doctor or making a public announcement. By the time she was certain it wasn't a false alarm and returned from the phone the head had appeared.

How many roles does a mother perform in a lifetime? Not all of them are pleasant. Here she was now, the unwilling midwife.

Consult as many books as you care to, they mean nothing. No amount of reading matter, no amount of forewarning can prepare you for your first baby. For many, the memory of the agony slips from the mind quickly. It wasn't like that for me. There was no praising to heaven for this act of creation, there were only curses on my lips. I didn't think, 'My God, this is a miracle, my own personal miracle. I Giveth Life'.

Unprepared as I was for the blood, the repulsion of the afterbirth, my most vivid memory is of the umbilical cord. I had seen similar created by man in plastic. But this had been made by God.

I don't remember if the baby was light or dark in colouring. But I do know that I questioned silently why it wasn't crying. Why it wasn't screaming its lungs out like I had seen on telly.

My baby. My little girl was DEAD.

I was so heavily sedated and naturally exhausted that I slept right through the next day. When I woke, as gently as she could Mum explained what happened. Somehow she had rid the house of guests, to enable the doctor to attend unobserved.And now in my presence she was fighting to keep her anxiety and sorrow to herself.

Fate, she explained, had given me another chance at life, another chance unburdened by a responsibility to another.

I knew that she was trying to give me comfort,that what she was saying was true. In that, had I decided to tell Stuart that I was pregnant we would have married and it was unlikely that marriage would have survived if my baby had still died? I knew that I was still too young for motherhood and should be 'grateful', but I worried whether I would ever be mature enough for such a responsibility, ever.

The next day I got up. Pulled on a dress, smoothing it down over my once-again flattened stomach, and went about my day, all emotions well hidden.

And Mum. She never mentioned it again. She just kept on loving me.

The Little Looker

Jacqueline Pilton

Once upon a time there lived a little girl in a little house with two wicked looking people she called her parents.

The little girl hated her parents, so at the first opportunity she looked out for a handsome prince.

When she found one, she married him and ran away from home. But soon, the handsome prince turned into an ugly toad and the little girl hated the toad prince like she had hated her parents. So much so, she ran away again, taking her baby with her, just for security in old age.

She soon found another prince, however. He wasn't handsome this time, but then handsome princes had brought her bad luck and, anyway, at least this one wasn't a toad.

They lived happily ever after for about a week, when unexpectedly the prince turned into a hideous vulture and tried to eat her baby. So the little girl ran away for the third time, but this time she wandered around for many years. She looked everywhere for princes and grew two inches smaller as a result.

She stayed in many lands but always the princes turned into toads or vultures.

At last she thought 'I've been very silly. I'll forget all about princes and just live quietly with my baby' (who was now a prince himself.)

Well you know what happened next? Yes, I bet you've guessed it, her baby prince very gradually started growing slimy feet and an ugly face just like his father.

The wee, tiny, little girl, by now had 'had it up to here' as they say, with toads, princes and vultures. What's more she hardly knew one from the other.

Well, there were no more places left in the world to stay and no more princes to stay with, so the little girl remembered her old parents whom she had hated long ago and she decided to return home to them — if only to get away from her toad-like son.

When she arrived at her parent's home it seemed bigger than she'd remembered it, but she stayed with her parents who looked different to her and she came to love them and shortly she grew a little taller so that she fitted the house nicely.

But the girl's parents were old and they soon died, so now whe had no one but herself and she lived in the house by herself for a long, long time, and grew bigger and bigger, until one day there was a knock on the door. It was the toad-like prince who was her son. He was cold and hungry, but still looked like a toad and even had a hint of vulture like his step-father, but the girl took him in and gave him food and shelter, even though she had to look at him over the breakfast table everyday and this put her off her food.

However, she forced herself to look, and the more she looked the more she noticed him becoming more beautiful. One day, he became so beautiful she loved him again and on that very day he left to continue on his travels. But the girl was not sad for long, for by now she was used to being alone and what is more, she knew now that when you look for beautiful princes, you find ugly toads, but if you stare at ugly toads, they become princes.

As she was thinking this ... there came a knock at the door. There was the handsomest prince she'd ever seen. She invited him in and they lived there together, until they both died. But never once did the girl look at him, and always wished him 'How do you do', over breakfast as if she'd never seen him before, and as if by tomorrow he'd be gone.

After she died she met lots of other princes and parents and toads and vultures and also new creatures she'd never seen before, but she never stared at one of them for too long and in any case, she found, that eventually, although they were all different, in a funny way they were all alike and it was too much bother sorting them out.

So, if she looked anywhere she looked at herself and she

looked at herself and looked at herself and she grew bigger than all the worlds and bigger than all the times so that now she had never been a little girl at all.

A Day of Rest

Joan Batchelor

She hitched the grizzling baby higher, to sit on her out thrust belly that bulged yet again with new life. Then she bent carefully to lift the full basket from the wet pavement. As she straigtened she caught sight of the ludicrous sun glasses she wore in the rain. The shop window distorted her reflection, the beehive hairstyle monstrous. The glasses hid the now purple eye from the curious ... yet they were not fooled.

The teething infant was sick with a puking heave that splattered the pointed toes of her sodden, shabby shoes. Her own stomach lurched at the smell that was acrid and curdled. The rain was relentless. Not pouring but a misty cold drizzle that seemed to penetrate the very marrow of her bones. She felt utterly sick and weary. Oh for the birth of this one so that she could have at least one day of rest. She frowned, the pushchair leaned against the bus stop, its wheels thick with black, greasy mud. It streaked her wet skirt...

Alan would be furious if his tea wasn't on the table when he got home from work. She sweated at the thought of his anger and his fists ... less than two years of these had almost quenched any thought of rebellion. Almost ... she added grimly ... not quite. Sudden tears made her sore eyes burn. She tossed back the wet hair, glaring.

The single decked, red and white bus jarred to a halt, splattering her with yet more mud. The baby howled, clinging like a monkey to her dark strands of hair. The squat conductor watched with folded arms as she struggled to get baby, shopping and the pushchair aboard safely...

'Come on ... come on ... we 'aven't all day,' he snarled. No one came to her aid, yet all watched tutting and muttering at her clumsiness, staring, probing to the raw flesh beneath the foolish sun glasses ... She flushed red and hot. Each whisper seemed loud, close to shouted.

'Shame ... at her age too ... silly girl ... can't tell 'em these days...'

'I blame her mother ... lettin' her marry a man like that...'
'Well ... she made 'er bed ... let 'er lie in it I say...'
'Pity for the kids I do say...'
'Her dad's such a nice man too...'
'All the same these days.'

The bus started with a jolt that threw her off her balance so that she tightened her grip on the baby and let fall the basket to roll oranges, potatoes and baby food cans about the floor of the bus. Hands grudgingly handed her them, item by item as she stood in the crowded bus, feet apart, baby under one arm, struggling with her purse as she tried to refill her basket. The baby screamed, purple and unattractive. Other mothers clutching their offspring turned away their eyes, in guilt or shame ... she hardly knew ... she swayed to the rough movement, it flung her from side to side like a disjointed puppet. Her hair plastered her face yet she had no hand to brush the irritating strands away.

She walked from the bus stop to the cottage, dragging the rusting pushchair behind her over the rocky path, crying with frustration. Six months ago she had lived with her parents, where she had fled from Alan in terror ... taking the baby with her. She thought of his charm, the green eyes flecked with gold, the deep clefts of dimples down his cheeks, the only man she had known...

'A boy needs a father...' he had said earnestly, 'I promise I will change...' He smiled as she returned home ... then hit her across the doorstep.

'Welcome home...' he had said coldly. Then made her pregnant.

The baby bellowed and the basket felt as if it were lengthening her arm. Rain ran down the glasses, blinding her so that she stumbled through puddles that filled her shoes.

'We can have one child and you, love,' her mother had said nervously, her red fingers twisting her apron, 'But there just isn't room for more … it was hard before … you know that don't you … your dad … he isn't a hard man … but…' She was eager, worried sick, trying not to see the fresh bruises, helpless before her daughter's suffering…

'He's not so bad you know…' her dad had towered over her bent head. 'Pays his round … needs to grow up a bit that's all. Did the right thing marrying you. Could have denied it was his.' She had nodded.

The wizened old lady next door to her house was in her doorway, despite the rain … she beamed at the soaked girl…

'Eh dear, there'a an' ol' day to be sure … been shopping is it? HE'S in, mind…' her treble voice faltered. The girl smiled with tight lips,

'Thank you Mrs Thomas. Don't worry … it'll be alright,' her heart all but stopped. Poor old lady, pity she wasn't deaf to the sounds through their stone walls. She saw the old woman's mouth tremble and said again,

'It will be alright love, you'll see…' The woman smiled faintly, her old eyes in some distant, brutal past.

The pain doubled her suddenly as she groped for her key. She leaned gasping against the door staggering as it was roughly opened from within. He had burst the buttons of his shirt over his chest again she noticed.

'Late again you bitch … where's my tea?' The muscles of his arms tensed as he held the door.

He towered over her, filling the doorway, as purple faced as his son. She longed to lean on his solidness and have those strong arms comfort and protect her.

'Have you been to see my mother again?' he yelled, blue veins were prominent and throbbing at his temples … 'I told you the old cat just tries to make trouble between us … you're to stay away … you hear?' She thought of his mother and her tumbling, crushed pride and blue, bewildered eyes. The hours that the woman spent over a stove, cooking disasters that sank in the middle that she disguised with gritty homemade cream. The rows when they went there. His aloof father.

Alan dragged the shrieking baby from her numb arms and dropped it into the big, black pram by the fireside. She emptied her basket swiftly, changed the baby as its bottle heated,

then washed her hands. Her feet felt squishy inside her soaked shoes, mud pushing up between icy toes. Alan raged on...

She lit the oven. There was a cooked casserole inside, not
that HE would have heated it, he would have thought that
far beneath his dignity. He was perplexed at her silent attitude. Her inwardness...

'Let me quiet the baby first, then we can have tea in peace,'
she said ... then more bravely, 'Will you put the kettle on
please?' He stared at her as if she had asked for the moon
with jam on ... but he put out his hand for the kettle, his
mouth tight.

She busied herself ... warming plates. The pain caught her
again so sharply that she cried out. She felt the wetness pour
hotly down her legs. Alan had plugged in the kettle and now
turned towards her, he stared at her with disgust, at her body
hunched over the stove and the red pool at her feet.

'Oh God ... that's put me right off my tea ... ' he blustered.
She took off the glasses that had collected puddles of sweat
around their frames. She trembled without control, sick with
lonely terror..

'I ... I'll have to go and lay down a minute...' she
whispered.

'What about the cup of tea?' he yelled.

'You make it...' she flashed, flinching from habit as she
did so ... He lifted his fist and then dropped it, muttering.
He banged two mugs around...

'Bloody woman can't even have a bloody baby without
a lot of ol' fuss...'

'Just marry him to give the baby a name ... you can divorce
him as soon as possible then ... I will have no bastards in
this house...' her father had raged. Sounded so easy then
... not so easy in practice. Over a year ago now, the boy was
eight months old and she was now five months pregnant
with threats of a pregnancy every year 'to cut out her
capers...' whatever that meant. It had been a grave error to
have told him that she had not been a virgin. Just that one
time ... long ago ... Alan had been incensed, he had
whispered over and over in her ear,

'You say that you love me ... yet you let him and you won't
me. How can I believe you?' She had drowned in the passion

of his gold flecked eyes. In her innocence she had thought he would have found out her indiscretion on their wedding night had she not told him ... She had wanted their relationship to hold honesty above all else, and had bred hatred. He hated women and feared men. She tried hard to understand why she had become his whipping post for this deepest hatred.

Upstairs the pain worsened, savage and consistent. She writhed on the unmade bed. Downstairs she heard him curse as something smashed to the floor and the baby wailed in protest at the noise. Utter terror was red behind her lids, beating to her pulse, punctuating her pain.

'Alan ...' she called, 'Get the doctor ... quickly.'

Alan climbed the narrow stairs and slammed down a half filled cup of dark brown liquid. His face was hard set.

'Jesus...' he exclaimed, 'Look at the bloody bed.'

She had trailed blood across the lino and spread it with mud onto the white sheets. The bed looked like a place of carnage. He thumped back downstairs and came up jangling a bucket.

'Here ... use this. I'll go and fetch the doctor.' He didn't hurry.

She twisted with the pain, gasping aloud and leaning over the bed. Facing her was the dressing table mirror and she grimaced at her reflection, her wet, rats-tails hair, the unhealthy pallor of her face, the brilliant bruising. She noticed her dirty feet with horror, she must wash them, what would the doctor think? Slowly, like a very old woman, she went downstairs. She looked in the pram, the baby chewed on his feet, dark eyes magpie bright. She was weary ... She took off her stockings and washed herself in cold water. Then she gathered up clean bed linen and the baby and even slower, made her way back upstairs.

With slowed down motions she made clean the bed, tossing aside the muddy, bloodied sheets. She used four sanitary pads and two pairs of cotton knickers, the blood still dripped. She undressed. She felt pride in her wash. One of her delights was to stand in the sun and watch breezes blow snowy nappies and sheets on the line. Such a small bit of happiness. Panting, she laid an old towel on the bed, over the bottom sheet. She lifted the baby from his cot; he was cold, the fire was out downstairs. He clung like a limpet, searching about with his mouth. He was such a good baby really. She held him until the pain doubled her, then placed him inside the bed. She squatted over the bucket, feeling the thick blood gush from her. Unnatural, lightening her head with its loss ... God, she was tired.

A car stopping outside made her leave the indignity of the bucket and crouch in bed, nightdress about her waist, a sheet covering herself.

She knew at once that the doctor noticed her eye. It stood out, a purple mass in her white face. He made no comment. He moved the baby to one side where it lay noisily sucking at fat little fingers. Alan had stayed downstairs. Sulking no doubt, she thought bitterly.

At some time during the next hour the midwife had arrived, ordering a sullen Alan to boil water, to pack a bag for the baby, to move himself...

'I'll have no nonsense with That one...' she had said to the doctor. With unbelievable gentleness she washed the girl's face until the pain had become past bearing, then she had busied herself, clucking like an old mother hen, muttering to the silent doctor as if the girl was deaf...

'His father was the same ... scum ... bad blood I say. Mind you, his mother was a silly woman to have spoilt the boy so ... used to hit her I hear ... her own son...' Her voice trailed off as the doctor met her eye. They were on their knees at the bedside, piecing together the mess of afterbirth very carefully with tweezers. They looked ridiculous. As if they were doing a complicated jigsaw. The baby held the girl's finger. She felt comforted by its active little body, but oh, so very tired.

The doctor straightened, then sat carefully down beside her on the bed. He patted her wet hand. She stared up at him with trusting eyes.

'The nurse is taking your baby to your mother's house. I'm afraid you have lost most of the afterbirth and the dead baby is still in there. We will have to remove it. I've sent Alan to phone for an ambulance.' He sounded calm. She felt nausea at the thought of her warm womb now a coffin. They both seemed to watch for some sort of reaction from her, yet all she felt was pain and tiredness once the nausea had passed. The midwife lifted the chuckling baby from the girl's side, loosening his firm grip on his mother's hair. She held him, crooning and smiling as he waved his chubby legs.

Alan carried her down to the waiting ambulance. She was barely conscious yet she noticed all the neighbours out in force. Gathering in the rain. Thank goodness I washed my feet, she thought as she saw her pink toes sticking out of the blanket. Alan seemed subdued. He held her carefully, smiling with an anxious frown at the crowd ... someone patted his shoulder in sympathy. Someone returned his smile. They all stared.

The fog of anaesthetic wore off. She felt like a deflated balloon. White, crisp uniforms passed. Someone wet lips that had cracked. Took her pulse. Her blood pressure. She was jolted about, unable to fall into the pit of painless sleep that her whole body craved.

HE stood by the bed, refusing a chair. He stared down at her. Hostile as she brushed back her hair with a weak hand.

'Christ ... you look a mess...' he said, 'It was another boy anyway, so it was for the best...'

Her eyes filled. A son ... she had lost a son ... A different kind of pain filled her chest until she felt it might burst. Alan looked awkward.

'I must go ... be late for work...' he muttered. Without another word he went, cold and forbidding. She held herself, mourning her son ... if only he had squeezed her hand, shared some of the sorrow. Everyone would think it for the best..yet it had been her son ... she moaned deep in her throat.

A nurse pulled the screen about her bed as a young doctor approached. He pulled out a chair and sat astride it. He wet his lips and spoke,

'Mrs Jones, I feel I must warn you that you must not have another child. In fact it would be most unwise to try.' He sounded as if he had been practicing his speech...'The ideal thing would of course be sterilisation, but your husband has refused to sign the form. I should like you to persuade him. Now I do realise that there are some difficulties within your marriage...' He flushed and looked away from her bruised face. 'Your private life is your own business, I am concerned about your health.'

The girl smiled mirthlessly. Persuade him? If only she could but reach him...

'He wants a daughter, doctor ... but I can see if he will wait...'

The doctor bent over and examined the contused eye pointedly. He stiffened his spine at the sorrow he read there. He had read it all before ... he would again. He felt helpless at a law which shielded these animals. No girl should belong to her husband. He was sickened by the pious cant of the church and lawmakers. He felt baffled, hurt, angry and helpless.

'Now look ... what use is a daughter if a mother dies at birth?' He stopped as she closed her eyes in resignation. Soon, but not soon enough would come the revolutionary pill now already available in many other countries ... until then his hands were tied. These men refused to use a sheath, there was not much else that was 100| sure, if that...

Her body was relaxing slowly, the warmth surrounded her. She felt safe ... her mind trembled with thoughts ... when had come the change in her? The spirit quenched as much by the attitude and ignorance of the day as by his ill treatment ... brute force ... where was love? tenderness? she could see a lifetime stretching ahead ... she gritted her teeth. Militant,was she? Puzzled for now, frustrated, her energy sapped by waves of weariness. Her son was dead. Somewhere inside her began a glow ... a slow-burning awakening ... she had lost her son ... but the burning felt good ... an elation that was stronger by the minute. It filled her with a kind of longing ... she stretched out her arms and legs feeling her body throb. Time for that much awaited divorce, and hang convention.

The bed held her close in a pure embrace. She thought of future daughters, strong and unafraid. Far off a baby cried. Wearily.

She slept ... just for now, clean and fragile ... she would enjoy her day of rest.

Comic Cuts

Helen Smith

Jo woke up fitfully, half willing her eyes to open and half reluctant to leave sleep behind. Beside her Catherine was leaning out of bed towards the radio, and familiar voices began to bring the room to life.

'I was having a funny dream.'

'What about?'

Jo did not reply. She was finding that she could climb back into the dream by hauling on the threads that it had left dangling around her. She could leave waking up to Catherine.

Through the wings a wedge of stage lay before her, all lights and a blur of movement. Her own thoughts were more electric still. Her haircut, catch that idea before it disappeared, the hairdressers, and what her mother had said when she got home. Good one. Next, quick, her glasses, wearing National Health specs and keeping them in her back pocket. Fine. And the next one.

'I'll make some tea,' said Catherine, scrambling out and allowing cold air to invade the spacious warmth of the bed. Jo felt one last prickle of excitement on her skin before the chill reached her. She curled up, unwilling to lose her thread.

Those eyes. Out of the darkness, pinning her to the stage. Expecting something of her, waiting for her to do something, to perform. Perform. It all came back. Planning her performance, back in the wings. The time had arrived. Those eyes, on her still, neither hostile nor supportive. She had swallowed her voice and her brain wasn't helping. What was her first line?

'I went to get a haircut,' her voice reached out across the stage, very loud in her own ears. She rejoiced in its strength, she was on her way.

The tray rattled pleasantly as Catherine brought in the pot, the milk and the cups. Jo patted Catherine's place in the bed, to welcome her back to it. When Catherine had poured the tea and turned to pass Jo her cup, Jo could see that she was smiling.

'What was this dream, then?'

'A great dream. I was a stand up comic, and it was just before I had to go on. I didn't know what I was going to say but all these ideas came to me for funny stories, and gags.

'Then I had to go on. It was a big place, dark beyond the edge of the stage and I could see all the eyes, waiting for me. Once I got talking it was all right. Then it was all over.

'You and I were walking along afterwards, down this street. It was late and quiet. I was high on how I was going to be a stand up comic and that was the problem of what to do with my life sorted out. You were being quiet. You know when you don't agree with me but don't want to say so, that's how you were.

'So then I asked what you thought of my act, and if you thought I'd make a good comedian, and you said no.' She wailed. 'That was you, beastly,'and she poked Catherine and wailed more at her smile.

That no. So matter of fact. The stark cold of the street was nothing to match the cold dark inside. An empty place was opening up inside her as she saw herself through Catherine's eyes, on that stage. Vain, inconsequential, embarrassingly bad. Perhaps just one more person in the audience had thought she was good? The hope died in mid-leap. There had been finality in Catherine's voice.

The Jo who was in bed warming her hands on a cup of tea recalled suddenly and with surprise that she had nothing in herself that at all resembled a stand up comic. People rarely laughed at her jokes, she lacked the touch. The last time she had got a laugh was when she'd been telling the Paul Daniels joke at that barbecue and had fallen off her chair because she was drunk. Bob had been laughing before she had finished the joke, before she even fell off her chair, because it amused him to hear someone telling an old joke so seriously.

There was no point in her trying to be a life and soul type.

'I'll tell you one thing though,' she said, moving across

the bed to lie right next to Catherine. 'In my dream just before I woke up, I was thinking I would carry on at being a comic, even though I hadn't made an instant success of it.'

'Which is something else,' she thought, 'that doesn't sound much like me.'

'Do you think I'd make a good comedian?' she asked wistfully.

'That's a good one,' said Catherine, and Jo laughed, and spilled tea on the sheet.

The Discovery

Qaisra Shahraz

In order to please his wife, Jamil had decided to clear up their spare bedroom. She was always reminding him of that room. It was a small room, which they hoped to set up as a baby's room, for their forthcoming child in six month's time.

Now as Jamil shifted himself around the contents of the room he found it hard work. Different types of boxes and bags had to be sorted, their contents rifled through, and quick decisions made as to what could be discarded and what ought to be kept.

Much of the stuff in this room belonged to his wife, Rubiya. There were magazines, books, clothes and bags of all sorts. There were three other carrier bags to sort out and then the room would be dusted and wiped clean. In fact, beautifully clean before his wife arrived home from her work. He looked at his watch. There was still an hour to go. He had plenty of time. In fact all of this would be finished in perhaps half an hour's time, and he could then start with the dinner. It was his occasional day off from work. He was definitely making the most of it in pleasing his wife. He'd vacuumed the entire house in the morning. Then he had worked on the bathroom later in the afternoon. And now for the last hour had been working in this room. Today the dinner would be ready for her for a change. He smiled to himself imagining her look of pleasure as she surveyed the work he'd done.

The box finished he grabbed another carrier bag. He peeped inside and put his hand in. Dust flew out. There were a lot of very dusty papers and pamphlets. He flicked through the papers — reading quickly, to see what they were about. Here was another paper, but this time he recognised his wife's writing. As his eyes followed the words on it, his mind froze.

Jamil threw the paper back in the bag as if it burned him, and stood up, his face set and his eyes glaring out of the window. He bent down and lifted the bag. Taking the piece of paper he'd just thrown in, he kicked the bag aside and left the room. He shoved the paper into his trouser pocket. He was going downstairs, and then he changed his mind and came up again. Pushing the door open, he entered his bedroom.

The first thing that caught his eyes was the framed picture of him and Rubiya as Bride and Bridegroom 'Dhullan' and 'Dhulla' on the dressing table. Jamil purposely walked to the dressing table and once there he flung the picture onto the floor. The glass frame broke into three pieces. He looked at them, but didn't bother picking them up. Rubiya's radiant, jewel-clad face stared back at him. He turned away.

He walked to the window and stared out in space, not seeing the green open field in front of him. He swore under his breath. He fumed. To think he had spent the entire day working away cleaning the house in order to please *her*. 'The filthy hussy' - the words came out again under his suppressed breath. Moving away from the window he flopped down onto the bed. He switched on the bedside radio. Thoughts and anecdotes whizzed through his mind. He wanted a distraction. Madonna's No. 1 hit didn't mean anything to him. He switched the radio off and pushed his face into the pillow. All the hints and thoughts which had meant nothing to him earlier now fell into place like a jigsaw puzzle. Now he understood why she didn't go to that wedding. The damned excuses she'd used. And he a blind fool, worshipping her for her gorgeous face, had played to her tune. He detested himself. Now he understood why she avoided some of her friends!

Jamil was still staring at the ceiling, he couldn't tell for how long, when he heard the front door open. That was *her*. He didn't move a muscle. Normally he would have raced down the stairs to greet her, to hug her. Not today. He heard her call him. Then again. No sound escaped his lips. Then she was clambering up the stairs. And was now in the bedroom. He needed time to think, to decide. He didn't want to see her face.

'Oh, here you are', Rubiya spoke over her shoulder, as she peeled off her outdoor coat, 'Because you didn't answer, I thought you had gone outside.'

Wordlessly Jamil got off the bed and went outside onto the landing, his hand balled inside his pocket, fingering the piece of paper. His hand clenched it. His wife was speaking again. 'Did you clean the small room then, Jamil?' she called. He was unable to prevent the retort that came out. 'Yes. Guess what I found there?' The words sounded rough and alien to his ears. They were laced with anger and bitterness. He pushed the door open and went inside the room.

Rubiya was lying languidly on the bed, flicking off her high stiletto court shoes. He looked down at her close cropped hair with brown highlights, her well-made face accentuating her regular well-formed features. She looked very attractive in the sleek maroon jump-suit hugging her body. Normally he would have been by her side on the bed by now. At the moment he was seeing her through the eyes of other men. The vision sickened him. God knew, how many men she had attracted with her looks, looks which nauseated him at the moment. Wasn't he himself allured by them. But whereas before he'd thought he was the only one entitled to admire her looks, now he wasn't so sure. There was definitely someone lurking about from her past, whom Rubiya had tantalised. Unable to bear the picture it conjured up in his mind he wanted to hit out.

Instead he drew out the piece of paper and flicked it down onto her chest. He wanted to erase that confident, self-possessed smile from her face. Shaking a curl from her eyes, Rubiya got up on her elbows and picked up the paper. As she recognised the paper and her eyes traced the words on it, the smile was whipped away, as Jamil had anticipated. The words, written by herself five years ago, stared back at her. She froze. She was living a nightmare. She'd always imagined her husband confronting her with her past deed, but never for the world imagined that her own hand would betray her. She looked again at the piece, the hateful words swimming before her eyes.

'My darling, Rashid,

I am ready to do what you suggest. I will leave home and my family in order to be with you. I will contrive a way in order to go away with you. I will meet you in the afternoon at 2.00 p.m. near the post office at the end of the road.'

Her heart was beating erratically. The self-assurance which was earlier etched on her features was there no more. She stared back at her husband. Jamil looked pointedly into her eyes. He didn't trust himself. He certainly didn't trust his tongue. He wanted to lash out at her, call her the horrible things that she was. He wanted to even do physical damage to her. He looked at her body again. It was soiled for him. He was the only one with whom she had a physical relationship with, but the thought of the other man, Rashid, being near her, was driving him insane. She was ugly, she was tainted.

He lashed her with his eyes. She felt hedged in. Between them stood another world — a world of Rubiya's past. Her past had caught up with her. She saw the hate and loathing imprinted on his face. She must make an effort to defend herself. She couldn't bear the look on his face. She got off the bed and flicked the paper in the basket. Her mind was still dizzy from this outcome.

'Oh, that letter was written while I was still at school. All girls were writing such letters in those days. And I did the same.' She finished lamely.

Jamil, however, had already left the room, banging the door behind him. The next minute she heard him go outside, and the car started to purr into action and away it was gone.

Rubiya sank onto the bed and covered her eyes with her hand. From a happy evening she was looking forward to had turned into a nightmare. Oh, god, he knew. For two years she'd made every effort to hide that stupid, lousy secret of hers. And here it was, now in the open. She'd always imagined Jamil's feeling of horror and revulsion, but somehow now that he knew it seemed much worse. She remembered the look in his eyes. He had looked at her as if she were something hideous. She hated that look. She'd never seen it before. Always he had looked at her if not with reverence, at least something near to it. Now she knew that look would never return.

He was a good husband. Unlike so many couples, they had an equal relationship. They'd had lovely times together, and she knew he adored her good looks. She caught sight of the broken picture frame. Somehow the action was symbolic. It meant he couldn't bear the sight of her. The broken pieces mirrored the tainted image that Jamil had of her now in his heart and mind. Her mind still reeled from the shock. To think, a small action could have such disastrous results. All she had done was to go away with a man for a day, whom she later detested. Nothing had come out of it and she'd returned. She hadn't even let him get within an arm's length of her. Who would ever believe her?

She braced her shoulders. She was going to make an effort to redeem herself in Jamil's mind and to save her marriage. She was certainly going to try. She would explain to him everything. She looked at the clock. She didn't know whether the dinner was made or not. But if it was not she would make it. She went downstairs into the kitchen and found it wasn't.

The next evening Rubiya was making dinner again. Jamil was out. He had not told her where he was going. Nor had she asked, fearing his earlier sarcastic remark. 'What is it to you where I am going? Unlike you I am not likely to go off with anybody.' Rubiya had flinched from his remark, hurt to her very soul. Normally if he made any sarcastic remarks she'd never let him get away with it. She would lash out immediately and lace her own remark with as much sarcasm as she could muster. Not this time, however. It was not her right, her priority. If she did, he would only taunt her as he had done last night.

She remembered the previous evening. She told him everything when he returned home. She might as well not have bothered. He was deaf to any pleas, her explanation. He was not affected in any way. The new spectacles through which he was viewing her weren't to be removed. They were well and truly stuck. When she mentioned 'dinner' he'd barked at her that he'd already had it elsewhere, but she needn't ask where. Again she had fumed inwardly, unable to retaliate. She didn't know how to react. She'd never been in such a situation with him before. That horrible deed was making her more and more vulnerable. If she called him, he didn't bother answering her. The table wasn't set for the breakfast. Nor was hers made. He had eaten and then departed for work, without even saying goodbye. At night he'd lain by her side, but made no effort to touch her. On the contrary she had the impression that if she touched him accidentally he would have flinched.

Did he hate her that much? She was still the same person. Surely he couldn't change that much towards her. Where was his love, his gentle, considerate ways? He hadn't changed! What was changed was the image of her in his mind and he had changed to suit that image. She hated the image he created of her in his mind, as a soiled wife, an image in which he had lost both respect and trust.

Her day at work was clouded by what had happened the previous evening. All day her mind dwelt on Jamil, on what he was thinking and how he was going to behave tonight. To say that she had not liked his mood last night was the understatement of the year. Her mind buzzed over remarks she could make in order to defend herself, if the situation arose. The situation didn't arise. He wasn't in when she got home. She waited patiently, prepared the dinner and then ate it by herself. Three hours ticked away. He still hadn't returned. Nor had he phoned her to let her know where he was. If he had done that at any other time, she would have been in a blazing temper by now, and would have flared at him the moment he entered the door. Now, however, she feared the repercussions, if she approached him about it. She was shaking with anger. In her mind she saw a picture of Jamil gradually turning into a tyrant and she herself gradually becoming more and more obsequious because of his discovery.

Rubiya shoved the plate away from her. She might as well have been eating sawdust. No! It couldn't be. It was a psychological blackmail. No person had the right to dominate another in such a way. The situation revolted her.

If Jamil stayed in this mood and taunted her whenever it suited him, she would be a silent sufferer always, taking the brunt of his anger, and unable to air her own.

No! she wasn't going to go through that again. She had too much pride. She wasn't made to be smothered under someone else's feet. She'd already been smothered enough. She wasn't going to relive the nightmare of three previous years spent at her parents. There she was made to suffer for her deed daily. Her mother, who never forgave her for what she had done or what she made them go through during those two fatal days made her a perpetual scapegoat for her anger. She was not to be trusted any more. Unless accompanied by either of her two sisters she was not allowed to go anywhere. Her mother feared that she might elope again and bring disaster upon them all.

Over the three years she saw her normal buoyant self being smothered under her mother's tyranny and the obsequious mantle she was forced to wear. In her mind there flashed a vision of her reliving those three years but this time for life, and with her husband. A shudder escaped from her spine. She loved her husband, and wanted to save her marriage there was no doubt about that, but not at the expense of her sanity, of her emotional survival. She was not born to receive her husband's taunts for the rest of her life, for a supposed crime. Life could not be so unfair. She tasted gall in her mouth.

With shaking hands, Rubiya pushed her plate aside and got up from the table. She turned away from the kitchen, without giving the dishes another glance. The pretty china plate perched on the edge of the table had no place in her mind. It could fall and break for all she cared. She banged the door behind her and went up to her room. She too could bang doors as much as she liked. In a strange way she felt better for it. She wasn't born to be locked up in a marriage where she danced to her husband's tune.

Almost mechanically she put on her coat and got her handbag. She left everything as it was and went downstairs. She was not sure what she was going to do, but she knew one thing — she was not going to spend this night in this house. She wasn't going to go through yesterday evening again. Opening the door she stepped outside. A blast of cold air attacked her face, the street lamps shining in the dark. She pulled the collar of her coat closer to her face and slammed the door behind her. Strangely, the fogginess she earlier experienced disappeared. Her mind was clear. She was back to her normal self; the self of her teenage years. She purposefully walked towards the garden gate. She had suffered enough for her crime. Tonight she would go to her parents', but later she would set up her own home, by herself if need be. Thoughts of her forthcoming baby didn't affect her. Setting up a home by herself would create another murmur in her community. She'd already lost everything, this action of hers in leaving her home and living by herself wouldn't cost her much. She braced herself for her parents' reaction when they found out she was abandoning her home, her husband and her marriage. Bitterness seeped through her. She didn't care a dime for what they thought. Nora Helmer's slamming of her house's door in Ibsen's *The Doll's House* came to her mind. She recalled the twittering of Claire Bloom in the screen version of the play. Her mind revolted from the picture of herself twittering around Jamil, dancing to his tune. She was a twentieth century Muslim Nora. A Nora who was slamming the door not only on her husband but also on her past.

Once on the road she hailed a taxi. When asked where she was bound, 'A turn round the whole city', she replied. The night, and its accompanying darkness did not bother her. A hysterical giggle rose in her throat. She imagined her parents' look of horror when they confronted her on their doorstep at 2 o'clock in the morning. The cord of convention was truly severed.

Fifteen Seconds

Joelle Taylor

Fifteen seconds was all that it took as the heavy velvet hair twisted out from her sinking head, knotting, tangling, groping for something or someone to cling on to: a lifetime of rehearsal and practice. The rotting tooth of a decaying branch sprang out from the bank and bit into her neck, dragging her further down, down into the black viscous stomach of the smooth river as it began to swallow and digest its prey.

'This is,' as voice said, 'the end of the beginning'.
And then the dreams began.

I

She was a child again. Long, flowing hair of golden innocence. And the smile: toothy and gummy and young. There were fields and flowers when she was a child, and every field was a desert, an oasis, a battleground, a fear filled jungle, a mountain, a river, a Canadian log-cabin, a playground for the imagination. Every day was a night or a noon in another place, in another time, in another person's body.

'Here we go round the mulberry bush, the mulberry bush, the mulberry bush, on a cold and frosty morning.'

A child's voice: 1 2 3 4 5. I'm playing hide and seek she thought. Games are like that: they prepare the innocent for the corrupt. Hide and seek, cat and mouse, follow the leader, follow the leader, follow the leader...

6 7 8 9 10. We play games all of our lives. Love and hate, War and Peace, and 'I'm not your friend anymore', and then, 'Make friends, make friends, never, never break friends, if

you do you'll catch the flu, and that's the end of you.'
Everybody plays and everybody wants to win.

11 12 13 ... Working up to shrieking fever measle pitch.
14 15 ... Coming ready or not. I'm not ready. NOT READY!

II

Pulled into adolesence and pop-socks and short skirts and
tight blouses and long warm day-dreams. Dragged away from
childhood and clarity and bound and tangled by the con-
straints of teenage confusion. 'O' levels,'A' levels, Honours
Degree, work, work, work: death. Silence. I don't want to
grow up anymore. I don't want to wear stiletto heels on my
mind and have a large, brown handbag in which I can store
my brain. Independence: not to rely on anyone else. I want
to be alone, but not lonely. I want to be free, but not ignored.
I want todream and feel and think.

I will be king and you will be queen. No, I will be queen
and you will be king. But who's going to buy the food. Who's
going to feed the bills, who's going to queue for more? Please
sir, who will queue for more? So there she was, drowning
before she'd drowned. Clawing at Hope instead of the
gripless river bank. Even then, the sides of Hope were slippery and difficult to grasp and clutch on to. They will say
the same again, she thought, they will say the same this time
that they said that time. This is only the physical proof of
the mental, emotional drowning. They will say: Suicide or
Murder? Silly. They are both the same. Suicide is murder by
the people who will not listen, who are too embarrassed by
the unusual nature of honesty in the statement, spoken or
silent, 'Help Me.'

III

People don't grow old: they just grow tired. Twenty-four
and already forgotten. Married and mis-managed with several
children at her breast to prove that she is a child no more.
'Here comes the bride, here comes the bride...' Sounded,

felt like the Death March four years, four children and four sleeping tablets a night onwards.

'Have you seen the price of bacon these days, Mrs Married to Him?' And she joined in, totally enthusiastic about bacon, flour, eggs, milk, cabbage and cheese, not to mention the unmentionable mushroom prices.

'I want the best for my children.' Totally forgetting that children are people and can only, must only, be guided and not controlled, not filled with second-hand morality. Had she forgotten that already? Still, she mustn't be philosophical when there were floors to scrub and smiles to smile.

Then one day she found one clue in her husband's 'Times' crossword, and found her brain. It was difficult to spot at first, shattered into several pieces: crouched between the dishes, sulking on the laundry, but the biggest piece was hidden in her husband's pocket.

'I want my mind back!' she exploded over the crossword to the impervious face before her.

'Give me back my mind. It is mine. I earned it, cooked for it, played with it, watched it grow out of shorts and into long trouses. Give it back to mummy'.

He smiled a smileless smile, 'but I pay the rent'.

That was that, whatever 'that' was.

IV

The letter said 'freedom' but it **felt like 'lost'. Unreasonable** behaviour, my lord, she wanted her brain back. She must be a lesbian, or a slag, or a closet Greenham woman, or a **vegetarian, or a communist or simply insane.**

'No!' she replied, 'I simply without my mind. Insane people are only the ones who are punched and feel the pain'.

'Divorce.' Next please. Kindly old judge. And then, husband and wife became children again, playing: 'Tug of War' with their seeds, their creations, THEIR children. She lost. The weaker sex. Still, there was always Sundays. Trembling visits to her offspring, laden with chocolates, comics, zoo trips, days at Southport, car rides and superficial happiness. It felt strange walking back into the house that she'd built up, to the children she'd brought up to be met by HIM and

the new Mrs Married to Him. He was always nice. Nice, nice,
nice ugly word. He was short and sweetex.

'How's life for you, then?' gloating, jeering, laughing
nicely.

'Life is MINE.'

Then there were the neighbours. What WOULD the
neighbours think? DO the neighbours think?

'She's gone now. Wasn't good enough for him. I told her
to buy 'Persil Automatic' and not that cheap stuff. But she
wouldn't listen. NOW look where it's got her.'

V

It got her herself. And her mind. And her hopes. And her
dreams. And her life.

The flatlet was in the city centre. Gone to pastures con-
crete, a plastic paradise. Cooking was a problem at first. She
cooked for four instead of one for she was one now. She
ate unhealthy, heart disease, fat and conceited food, fresh
from the freezer, and watched television. The 'Likely Lads'
— Apt: 'What happened to you, whatever happened to me?
What became of the people we used to be?'

There was also a mirror. Mirror, mirror on the wall, who
will answer when I call, who will care and who will hate.
Who willclap when I've washed my dinner plate? Two eyes,
a nose, a mouth, ears and eyebrows.

'But it isn't me.' There must be more to me than that ex-
terior, veneer, wall, shrouding that which I call me, 'there
must be'.

Drowning was an accident. Isn't it always? She slipped
picking flowers at the bank.

'...a pocket full of posies, we all fall down.'

She'd lived like that. A pocket full of poses. Script with
stick replies and emotions. A pocket full of poses.

VI

Her body lay on the cold, moist slab, in the white, white,
whiteness of the mortuary lab. There was a faint hum of
muffled voices and the mumbling of uncertain footsteps. The

sheet was dragged back off her stiff face to reveal carefully sewn-down eyelids and a bulging blue mouth.

'Yes, that's her. Her that was married to me.' Sliced through the silence. 'How did she...?'

'Death by mis-adventure: drowning. Down by the reservoir. So many things under the water to hold you down. Old prams, bicycles, scrap cars, clawing, disembodied trees ... so many things to hold you down.'

'Did she feel anything?'

'Nothing: It was all over in fifteen seconds, Sir. All over in fifteen seconds.'

Andante

Di Williams

The slight smell of woodsmoke stirred childhood memories as she crunched through the leaves to the wooden gate. The late afternoon sun was golden on the horizon. It had been streaming across her aching eyes on the coach. That had been only 20 minutes ago — but it felt as if a whirlwind and at least a week had passed. Last night, the party, music played into the windy darkness, the huddling together, farewells intoned in the morning and then recently in the coach. Now she stood on unmoving ground. Why did it always feel like a culture shock?

Her brother-in-law came to the door and broke her train of thought, as he reached out for her saxophone case.

'Anne's just got the kettle on. You must be starving.'

'Spitting feathers, more than starving.'

He looked puzzled as he turned. She had meant she was thirsty. Wasn't it a Yorkshire expression? It must be Scouse, then. Anyway, she thought it was a good description.

'Kids are in the garden,' Anne called from the kitchen.

She hesitated before undoing her anorak. There were hangers on the hooks on the wall, most of them with coats of large and small sizes on them. Anne was always more methodical than she was, who usually hung hers over the nearest chair. Underneath her quiet observation, a twinge of guilt. No, she must fight that, as a woman with every right to her own lifestyle.

Danny burst in on her as soon as she reached the kitchen.

'We got a tape from the telly. Mum says we can show you. There was a lot of people dancing and — '

'There was a bonfire,' interrupted his sister.

'No, not the bonfire tape, the one about Molesworth…'

'I mean that one. They had a little fire. To keep warm.'

'And they was all in a line and then JUMPIN and SINGIN LOUD ANDANTE WAS — '

'ANTEWAS PLAYIN! WASN'T YOU?!!!'

'Was I?' she asked, looking at Anne. 'I didn't know it was filmed.'

'Danny spotted it. We only got the tail end, on the news programme.' Anne waited till her husband had gone into the garden. 'On the telly, eh? Little Jane kept saying it was you, then we played it back and I'm sure it is.'

'You got a stripey hat on,' said Jane.

Yes, those eyes smiling proudly had spotted her borrowed hat. Pity she'd given it back — it would confirm something to her niece. Aunts could be on T.V. They could also break the law of trespass, cut fences, have a whale of a time —

'We could show it you after tea, couldn't we, love?' — this was to her husband, as Anne's voice took on a placatory note. 'Sorry it's a bit fiddly, but it's at the end of the Saturday film.'

Anne had let her sister know, subtly, that she hadn't yet shown the video recording to her husband, and there was an uneasy tension in the way she started laying out the plates on the table, not looking up from the task.

He didn't say anything about it while they were putting the two children to bed. She could see her brother-in-law was frowning with the effort of a struggle — adapting to some new perceptions of her identity, doubtless.

Things take time to digest. Easy does it, stay quiet, she told herself. They'd always joked about her going to women's conferences. How much had her sister prepared him for this evening's shock — the film of her with the sax round her neck, Marie's arm round her shoulder, cheek to cheek swaying in the line? She didn't know they had T.V. cameras — you didn't often see a demo on T.V. The edge of the crowd — probably because they were playing music — and why not? She felt a stubborn glow of pride.

It was undercut by his tone in the opening question. 'You been living down in the peace camp or what?'

Anne cut in, 'You only go down to play on the big demos, don't you?'

Don't apologise for me, she thought angrily.

'You have to be careful,' he said. 'People say the women are a lot of lesbians.'

The gaping chasm of silence — both sisters were blushing.

No, she had to break through this barrier of fear. Better let it be faced now, than some time in the future.

'Yes, a lot of us...'

During the impact of her words, she had again the impression of a world of movement she had just left. Memories of walking, laughing together, words whose meaning was understood quickly, the phrases of music answering other instruments, then blasting out in a glorious chord.

She blinked at the room in her sister's house. Silence; the shock of a different world.

'I don't understand you. Surely someone like you wants to settle down...'

He wanted to believe in his good image of her, and he didn't want her to let him down.

'You get on great with the kids. Surely you want —'

'I love children, yes. Why not.'

Maybe one day — but she didn't go into that.

'I'm sure Anne worries about you.'

She was sure Anne knew her better than that. Anne was frowning a little. She would be worried about her husband, as if he were a boy she was protecting. Careful, no bitterness, she thought, it's been a strain. He is taking it better than some.

He was saying something, rousing her to stop speculating.

'And neither of us will say anything to anybody, will we, Anne?'

And she was trying to say, I've come out.

What do you do? Do you blow your top and tell your family, 'I'v stopped pretending!'? Do you get angry, and say, 'It is o.k., not illegal, never has been'? Do you shrug and take all the responsibility yourself, so that people can say what they like, you tell your family you can cope.

You can't cope, though, with what people in Sheffield will

say to that family when you're not there, she realised. She saw it was his responsibility to deal with that.

Softly, softly. Don't throw the baby out with the bathwater. The start of an education here. The children had seen 'Ante' on an anti-nuclear rally. A thing they'd be bound to want to talk about. Don't quarrel at this point.

Maybe she and Anne were too cautious, compromising. For a quiet life?

Don't rush, she decided, as she looked through their record collection for something for a more peaceful mood.

Anne came and found a record of jazz piano played by Thelonius Monk. Her husband had always fancied he belonged to the beatnik generation, she once said. They sat round the mock-coal fire in a time-warp, slower, safe and relatively cosy.

She was tired after the journey. Plenty of time tomorrow for the rush of her own life, on her own ground.

For the time being, she played along at walking pace.

Be a good girl

Ailsa Cox

Sundays were the long days at Grandma's. Every quarter of an hour, the clock would chime the first laborious notes in an endless sequence. The clock was dark and massive, like the huge gothic dresser and the piano that nobody played. Sun and Moon smiled at me from the tall clock, but that was a grandfather clock and Grandad was dead.

I wasn't allowed down from the stiff-backed chairs until everyone had finished. So I kept my eyes on the china shepherdesses and dogs caught on the many high ledges. In summer, the dust was trapped by sunlight, freckled through the crumbly lace curtains. Everything smelt of mothballs. When I couldn't eat, I'd sit waiting for the spidery fingers to edge along V, X, I. There was no proper time on the clock, only V, X, I. There was no TV, no wireless, no one to play with. If I had my new bouncy beachball I'd send it as high as the real moon and sun. The little dogs laughed. But since I couldn't run, I sat.

I watched the patterns in the parched crockery, on the yellowed wallpaper, on the stitched antimacassars and doilies. There was a lady, Mary, Mary, her face covered by a poke bonnet among the lupins on the firescreen. The copper kettle cast the shadow of a long-necked beast. Many islands were mapped on the dark red carpet; there were plenty of secrets in that chill, airless room.

Whenever I went to Grandma's, I wore my best frock, the one Granma bought for my birthday. There were always layers of nylon caught at the waist, sometimes pink, sometimes powder blue. It was the dress I was wearing in the framed photograph on the dresser, the only colour picture, in between the wedding and army photo's.

As Mummy jerked my hair into an elastic band, she'd say, 'Now have you been? Are you sure you've been? You'd best go again, to be on the safe side. Now try and keep yourself nice,' she'd say, pulling the hem of my coat straight. 'Don't forget to say thank you,' she'd say, twisting round from the front seat of the car. You'd scarcely know it was Mummy on Sundays. Her lips were glazed with red, her figure squeezed inside a tight-fitting suit.

As we walked through the gate, she'd still be brushing loose threads and dandelion wings from my shoulders. But once we were inside all the grown-ups ignored me.

They were all sat round the table — Auntie Violet, Auntie Florence, Auntie Gertrude, and then the next generation, Peggy, Betty, Marge, by the side of their silent other halves.

A voice would clatter with the cutlery: 'This weather doesn't suit me. The sun gives me a shocking headache.'

Or, if it was raining, the conversation was rheumatics. Some one would get up to close the curtains or shut a door against the draught.

It was during one of these drawn-out moments, as a chair creaked and feet padded, that I felt my bladder expand as slowly, as distinctly, as a voice inside me.

'Mummy...'

Mummy was sipping the thin soup thoughtfully. She seemed not to hear me. 'Mummy, mummy...' I touched her sleeve. 'Mummy, I want to go.'

She shushed me, looking round without turning her head. 'You'll have to hold it till we get home.'

'I can't. I feel bad.' My voice was rising. Still no one looked at me. 'I feel poorly, Mum.'

'Be a good girl. Just behave yourself till we get home,' she hissed. 'Haven't I told you, you can't go round people's houses asking to use the toilet.'

The soup bowls were cleared and the plates handed round - cold, fatty lamb with three boiled potatoes, one and a half for the child.

'Eat a little bit. Just try, there's a good girl. Grandma goes to a lot of trouble.'

I tried to eat, because the horrible feeling of eating would be worse than the other horrible feeling. If I ate all the fat,

Grandma would fetch out a boiled sweet from the bottom of her musty handbag. But instead of making me forget, the food made me feel worse, as if my whole body was bursting with wee. I thought of the seven times table, which was always worse than the sixth; then the divide by, harder than times; and in pound, shillings and pence, too. Then I thought hard about the nastiest things I could remember, like the big girl who waited outside school sometimes, or chickenpox or the dead cat with flies in its gums. These thoughts took me from II to XI, from pale brussel sprouts. But there was still washing up to go, cups of tea, whist, the drive home.

Mummy was in the kitchen washing up. I tugged at her pinny, but her back wouldn't turn.

One of the old trembly aunts patted my head. 'Aren't you a big girl now! And how are you enjoying school?'

'I want to go,' I said in a small voice.

The auntie continued in her loud voice: 'And are you a good girl for the teachers, Marietta? That's nice!' She had a pink tube in her ear. Another auntie couldn't eat cake, it was too rich for her. Another one gave me half crowns in sealed envelopes.

I went to the bottom of the stairs and looked up into the secret core of the house. No one would know if I slipped up to the toilet. But I couldn't. It was dark. Grandma slept there, and I was scared of Grandma. There were hairs on her face. She smelt all dusty.

I sat on the steps, my face deep in my nylon skirts.

When we got home, Mummy would run into the house, stumbling over the Yorkshire terrier. 'This girdle's killing me.' She'd kick off her high heels, fall into a chair and call out: 'Did you hear her showing off about that motor? It's all on tick, you know. They've no money of their own. They're all show. I don't know why she married him. He's common as muck. She could've had anybody when she still had her figure. Four doors! I know damn well they only make them with two...'

She'd pull me to her sharply, to get the buttons and ribbons undone. When the ice cream van tinkled in the street, she'd say, 'Alright then, just a small one, for being a good girl,' and I'd skip outside with twopence in my hand.

'Watch the traffic!' she'd shout, and then resume in a low, adults's voice, 'it's about time somebody did something with Auntie Violet. Did you see her with the peas?'

And I'd be away down the street like a bouncing ball. But not this time. The doors would be locked.

With my eyes shut, I could've been anywhere. The nylon was sand on my cheeks. The skirts rustled like the seashore. It was easy to pretend. The anger would break on me, but not now, later. I need not think about it now. I could enjoy the wet warmth pulsing through my knickers. Then I heard distant chimes moving into sequence, slowly at first and then with insistence. I never looked at the Sun and Moon again.

Biographies

Su Andi

When I first took up my pen and commenced to write
about my childhood, I did so purely for personal interest.
That my trials and tribulations would give testament to that
which has been endured by other Black women, I never considered. Especially women like myself whose life had come
forth from a black-white relationship.

Joan Batchelor

Former paid worker at Commonword, Welsh and proud
of it, Woman and loving it, Mother, Writer and general
dogsbody at Oldham Tec', on the catering side, Secretary of
a newly formed writing group based at Shaw, called Oldham
Wordsmiths. Have had several poems and short stories
published and have a great many more ...

Dorothy Byrne

I'm a journalist living in Manchester. I write very short
stories and poems about things I find ridiculous. This means
I usually write about men.

Ailsa Cox

I was born in 1954 in Walsall, West Midlands. Now I live
in Manchester with my nine year old son. Stories of mine
appeared in Commonword anthologies, like: Nothing Bad
Said and Home Truths; and in Critical Quarterly, Writing
Women and Stand One (Gollancz, 1984).

Rhoda Lamb

I am a housewife, who hasn't been writing long. I concentrate mostly on monologues and children's poems. I write late at night, to avoid being distracted by the telly and other things. Writing is an enjoyable pass-time, when you write your mind is on your work and nothing else.

Olivia Michael/Alice Sky

Is 27 years old and a single parent, studying English at Leeds University. She has written on and off since childhood, more continually in the past five years. After completing her degree she hopes to make a living from various kinds of writing and activities connected to it.

Jacqueline Pilton

Drama lecturer, actress and director, performing and teaching under the name of Jacky Tindsley. Has written children's theatre, sketches and one-women shows. Is currently writing poetry and articles for a forthcoming magazine emphasizing an individual spiritual approach for day to day living. Aged forty and has a son of twenty. Interested in metaphysics; growing indoor plants and working with the mentally handicapped.

Qaisra Shahraz

Born in Pakistan, and now living in Manchester for the past 19 years, has been writing since she graduated from Manchester University. She joined Commonword's Womanswrite workshop during her maternity leave, and from the encouragement she received from other members, she produced a small collection of short stories with a particular 'feminist' flavour. Before the stories, she wrote factual articles, three of which were published in 'She'. Currently, she is a lecturer at a local community college, teaching adults, and is working on a children's novel. She finds that she can write best under pressure and in unusual settings.

Helen Smith

Is in her early thirties and makes her living as a teacher. She began writing short stories at WEA writing classes and is now working on a science fiction novel.

Peri Stanley

I'm from the Midlands but living in Manchester now. I've been writing short stories for several years, but now I'm working on a novel.

Joelle Taylor

Is a 19 year old student, originally from Accrington in Lancashire, working for a degree in the Visual and Performed Arts at Kent University. She has been involved in writing performance poetry and prose for three years, struggling through the enlightening atmosphere of Working Men's Clubs and polite applauses to major feminist events. She believes that poetry lies within the message of the wor, and not within the words themselves. Her writing spans over a wide range of issues, from sexual abuse to general hints on how to deal with drunken menopausal males on Saturday evenings. Read on.

Kate Thomas

As a teenager my reading matter consisted of 'Jackie' stories, which I knew were true, and horror stories, which I hoped were. These have been the two main influences on my writing, and I think it shows in this story, which is either a romantic horror story or a horrible romance.

Alison Thorpe

I'm from London originally, but have been living in Manchester for three years now. I am concentrating on a novel, presently.

Liz Tolan

Born 1948, Bradford, West Yorkshire. After school, Art College and various jobs, slid into domesticity, gained spouse and three sons. 'Unemployed.' Member of a women's writing group. Have difficulty fitting writing into conventional forms, so attempting the opposite. Working on novel (ie quite a lot of pages) concerning a sheep.

Di Williams

From Whalley Range, Manchester, has been writing since adolescence. She has been a teacher of adult literacy, and started coming to Womanswrite workshops in Common- work in 1982. She is a songwriter and is beginning to make a living as a musician.

About Commonword

Commonword is a non profit making community publishing co-operative producing books by writers in the North West and supporting and developing their work. In this way Commonword brings new writing to a wide audience.

Over a period of ten years Commonword has published poetry, short stories and other forms of creative writing. HOLDING OUT is the first title published under the **Crocus** imprint. Forthcoming books include a collection of work by Black Writers, *Black and Priceless*; *She Says*, a volume of women's poetry; and *Now Then* — a book of creative writing with a local history theme.

In general, Commonword seeks to encourage the creative writing and publishing of the diverse groups in society who have lacked or been excluded from the means of expression through the written word. Working class writers, black writers, women, and lesbians and gay men all too often fall into this category.

To give writers the opportunity to develop their work in an informal setting, Commonword offers a variety of writers' workshops, such as Womanswrite, the Monday Night Group, and Northern Gay writers.

Cultureword, which is a part of Commonword and which acts as a focus for Black writers, organises the Black Writers' Workshop. Cultureword also co-ordinates *Moss Side Write* magazine, and a writing competition for Black Writers. A full-time worker is promoting Black Women's writing.

In addition to writers' workshops and publishing, Commonword offers a manuscript reading service to give constructive criticism, and can give information and advice to writers about facilities in their immediate locality. 'Writers Reign' magazine contains both information and new writing.

Commonword is supported by North West Arts, the Association of Greater Manchester Authorities, the Commission for Racial Equality, and Manchester City Council.

The Commonword/Cultureword offices are at Cheetwood House, 21 Newton Street, Piccadilly, Manchester. Our phone number is (061) 236 2773. We would like to hear from you.

If you've enjoyed reading Holding Out, *why not try some of our other recent books?*

Poetic Licence

Poetic Licence is an exuberant and bubbling brew of poetry from a diversity of poets living and working in Greater Manchester. Their work celebrates the many pleasures of poetry — from the serious and intense, to the playful and humorous.

This book contains work from some exciting new poets. There's writing from the Black Writers' Workshop, and Northern Gay Writers, as well as from 'Chances' — a group of disabled and able-bodied writers, and performance poetry from Stand and Deliver. Peter Street writes movingly of old age and disability, whilst Anne Paley looks at life in the '80s as a woman, there's poetry in patwa from Patrick Elly, and short witty pieces from Gary Boswell.

"There are many different emotions and moods to be found within these pages and, read in its entirety, the whole volume is disarmingly powerful … Excellent value for money"
(CITY LIFE 20/11/1987).
£2.50   208 pages   ISBN 0 946745 40 4

Between Mondays
The Monday Night Group

This collection of poetry is the latest book from Commonword's Monday Night Group. It brings together some promising new writers with plenty to say about life in the city, sexuality, Catholicism and many other subjects.

'A Northerner's Nightmare' describes the horror of a Salford lad lost on the London tube; 'Asleep in The Afternoon' takes us back to schooldays; 'Sideshow Sexuality' compares an adolescent girl's experience with the life of the fairground. This is just a small selection from a wide ranging anthology, which stretches from ranting to romance, and from childhood to old age.

"By publishing this book, Commonword has encouraged writers who might not otherwise have put pen to paper, who have valuable lives to share with us"
(ARTFUL REPORTER Dec/Jan 1987/8).
£2.50   104 pages   ISBN 0 946745 35 8

Liberation Soldier
Joe Smythe

What should poetry address itself to in the 1980s? Joe Smythe gives his own answer in this collection of recent work. Using a variety of styles, he explores the discontents and disturbances of the times, from inner city riots to apartheid in South Africa.

Joe Smythe also takes a fresh approach to more traditional poetic themes, such as love, time passing and the appreciation of the natural world. Running through all his work, though, is a streak of satirical humour, which crackles away even through the most serious of these well-crafted poems.

"Joe is a poet ... with a cutting edge. He writes with a sting, sometimes with ironic humour about what he knows best — the effect on him of living in the '80s and the way he sees it affect others"
(MANCHESTER EVENING NEWS).
£2.50   84 pages   ISBN 0 946745 25 0

Autobiography

Australian Journal: Alf Ironmonger   60p
In 1946, off the coast of South Australia, two young shipmates decide to jump ashore. This is their tale...
ISBN 0 946745 01 3   64 pages

Dobroyed: Leslie Wilson   £1.20
The unique inside story of one person's experience of a year spent in an approved school.
ISBN 0 950599 74 3   142 pages

Fiction

Nothing Bad Said £1.20
A collection of short stories by fourteen writers, dealing with issues and situations that affect all our lives.
ISBN 0 950997 6 X 96 pages

Marshall's Big Score: John Gowling £1.20
A book about a love affair, played out against the backdrop of the gay scene in London, Liverpool and Manchester.
ISBN 0 946745 03 X 76 pages

Turning Points: Northern Gay Writers £2.95
This collection of short stories and poetry explores moments of crisis — turning points — in the lives of a variety of characters, with various different conclusions...
ISBN 0 946745 20 X 120 pages

Poetry

Hermit Crab: Di Williams 30p
Using the imagery of the sea and the seashore, these poems tell of a daughter's journey towards independence.
ISBN 0 946745 15 3 28 pages

Consider Only This: Sarah Ward 30p
A selection of poems which captures the atmosphere of moorland, cotton mills and small town life.
ISBN 0 946745 04 8 28 pages

High Living: Ruth Allinson 30p
In these poems, Ruth Allinson casts a critical eye over social injustice and female exploitation.
ISBN O 946745 00 5 28 pages

Diary of Divorce: Wendy Whitfield £1.00
Wendy Whitfield reflects on the breakdown of her marriage in a series of poems and cartoons.
ISBN 0 9505997 7 8 28 pages

Forthcoming Titles

Black and Priceless £3.50
A collection of short stories and poems that reflect the power of Black ink!
ISBN 0 946745 45 5 Publication date: 8th June 1988

She Says £2.95
Fact and fantasy combine in this compelling selection of new poetry by women writers.
ISBN 0 946745 50 1 Publication date: 1st September 1988

Now Then £2.50
Memories of living and working in Greater Manchester, from after the Second World War up till 1980 — history with a difference!
ISBN 0 946745 55 2 Publication date: 3rd November 1988

Order Form

Title	Price	Quantity
Poetic Licence	£2.50	....
Between Mondays	£2.50	....
Liberation Soldier	£2.50	....
Australian Journal	£0.60	....
Dobroyed	£1.20	....
Nothing Bad Said	£1.20	....
Marshall's Big Score	£1.20	....
Turning Points	£2.95	....
Hermit Crab	£0.30	....
Consider Only This	£0.30	....
High Living	£0.30	....
Diary of a Divorce	£1.00	....
Black and Priceless	£3.50	....
She Says	£2.95	....
Now Then	£2.50	....

Please send a cheque or postal order (made payable to Commonword Ltd) covering the purchase price plus 25p per book postage and packing.

Name (block letters) ___________________________

Address: ____________________________________

____

_____________________ Postcode ______________

Please return to: Commonword, Cheetwood House, 21 Newton Street, Manchester M1 1FZ.